KU-559-224

PANHANDLE DRIFTER

DP SPR

Please return / renew by date shown.
You can renew it at:
norlink.norfolk.gov.uk
or by telephone: 0344 800 8006
Please have your library card & PIN ready

JAN 6TH 2012 3/11

WRW

17.

JAN 25TH 2012

06 SEP

D23

NORFOLK LIBRARY
AND INFORMATION SERVICE

NORFOLK ITEM

30129 061 217 957

PANHANDLE DRIFTER

When ex-lawman Jack Nelson drifted into the Texas Panhandle valley, little did he realize that he was about to be embroiled in a battle between unscrupulous rancher Willard Duff of the Box D and the six setters whose homesteads lined the river bank. Duff was determined to take over the whole of the land in the valley for his range, even if it meant resorting to murder, so he enlisted the help of Quincy Daley's outlaw gang. With the odds so heavily stacked against them would Jack and the home-steaders stand a chance in hell of thwarting the rancher's plans?

PANHANDLE DRIFTER

by

Alan Irwin

Dales Large Print Books
Long Preston, North Yorkshire,
BD23 4ND, England.

British Library Cataloguing in Publication Data.

Irwin, Alan
    Panhandle drifter.

A catalogue record of this book is
available from the British Library

ISBN   1-84262-187-4 pbk

NORFOLK LIBRARY AND
INFORMATION SERVICE

SUPPLIER	MAGNA
INVOICE No.	IO47665
ORDER DATE	25-2-11
COPY No.	

First published in Great Britain 2001 by Robert Hale Limited

Copyright © Alan Irwin 2001

Cover illustration © Faba by arrangement with
Norma Editorial

The right of Alan Irwin to be identified as the author of this
work has been asserted by him in accordance with the
Copyright, Designs and Patents Act, 1988

Published in Large Print 2002 by arrangement with
Robert Hale Limited

All Rights reserved. No part of this publication may be
reproduced, stored in a retrieval system, or transmitted in any
form or by any means, electronic, mechanical, photocopying,
recording or otherwise without the prior permission of the
Copyright owner.

Dales Large Print is an imprint of Library Magna Books Ltd.

Printed and bound in Great Britain by
T.J. (International) Ltd., Cornwall, PL28 8RW

ONE

When Jack Nelson rode out of New Mexico Territory into the Texas Panhandle he had no fixed destination in mind. For some time he had been wandering aimlessly through Kansas, Colorado and New Mexico Territory in an effort to forget the tragedy which had so grievously blighted his life.

He was a man of thirty years, tall, well built and clean-shaven, with dark hair showing from underneath the brim of his Texas hat. A good-looking man, there was an air of gloom about him as, slightly hunched in the saddle, he rode on in an easterly direction.

Two days later, riding through a hilly area about thirty miles from the border with Indian Territory, he entered a ravine which lay in his path. A little way ahead he could see an old shack standing close to the steep wall of the ravine. Not far from the shack a mule and a burro were grazing, but there was no sign of their owner. A small stream ran along the bottom of the ravine.

Jack rode up to the shack and called out, but there was no response. He looked inside. It was empty. Continuing his ride up the ravine he was expecting to see a prospector somewhere close by. Ahead, on his left, he could see that a section of the wall of the ravine had collapsed, leaving a large pile of debris at its foot.

Riding past the pile, he glanced at it and could see that the fall was recent. As he was turning his head to look up the ravine again, the slightest of movements on top of the pile caught his eye. He dismounted, and walked up to the heap of rubble, which consisted of a mixture of earth and rock fragments of various sizes. He closely inspected it.

Projecting from the top of the pile was a bloody finger which, once again, moved slightly and caught Jack's attention. Quickly, he started removing the rubble to expose first the hand, then the arm to which it was attached.

It was some time, even with the help of a shovel which Jack found lying nearby, before the whole of the body was exposed. It was that of an elderly man, short and bearded, with a deep cut on the side of his head which had been bleeding profusely. The man was breathing but appeared to be unconscious.

Then, as Jack was bending over him, his eyes opened. He looked up into Jack's face, then at the rubble around him.

'Who're you?' he asked, looking up at Jack again. His voice was faint.

'Jack Nelson,' Jack replied. 'You hurt bad?'

'Hiram Benson,' said the injured man. 'I'll let you know in a minute.'

In gingerly fashion he moved all his limbs, one by one, then felt his chest and ribs. Finally he put his hand up to the wound on his head and felt it.

'Looks like I'm lucky,' he said. 'I couldn't

move underneath that pile and I was running out of air to breathe. The worst things I've got are a bad ache in the head from that cut and a pain in the ribs. When that lot came down on me and I felt a big piece of rock hit my head I sure thought I was a goner. And all because I took my pick to a piece of rock sticking out of the side of the ravine.'

With Jack's help Benson rose to his feet and stepped clear of the rubble. Then, waiting until a severe attack of dizziness had abated, he walked slowly along to the shack and sat down on a rickety chair inside.

'Let me tend to that cut,' said Jack.

'I'd be obliged,' said Benson. 'There's plenty of bandages in that box in the corner, and some water in that pan on the stove.'

Jack cleaned the head wound and bandaged it. Then he felt the rib area.

'You breathing all right?' he asked.

'Same as usual,' Benson replied.

'Don't seem like there's anything broken,' said Jack. 'I'll slap some bandaging round you and we'll see how it goes.'

When he had finished he helped Benson over to one of the two bunks in the shack, and the prospector lay down.

'I reckon,' said Jack, 'that you'd better rest up for a while to let them wounds heal. I'll hang around for a while till you're feeling better.'

'If you hadn't happened by,' said Benson, 'I'd have cashed in for sure. I was jammed in tight under that fall. Just couldn't have got out on my own. I'm taking you up on that offer of yours to stay on for a spell, so long as you ain't expected somewhere else.'

'I'm expected nowhere,' said Jack, and for the next two weeks he fixed the meals for himself and Benson and attended to the prospector's wounds. At the end of the two weeks Benson thanked him and told him he was fit to fend for himself.

'I'm going to start work again tomorrow,' he told Jack. 'Gold ain't never been found around here, but I've got a feeling that there's some hidden away in this ravine if only I can find it. I figure on staying around here for a while.'

Jack took his leave of Benson the following day, just after noon. As the prospector watched Jack ride off to the east he realized that he knew no more now about the stranger who had helped him than he had when they first met. He wondered who the taciturn stranger was and where he was heading.

Three hours after leaving Benson, Jack rode into a valley and shortly after found himself approaching a homestead located on the south bank of the river he had been following. He hesitated, first intending to pass the homestead by, then deciding to call in and ask for directions to the nearest town.

There was, he thought, as he casually eyed the place, a slight air of neglect about it, even though the house and barn were obviously well-built structures, and the corral railing and pasture fence were stout and in good repair.

As he rode up to the door of the house, it opened and a woman stepped out, followed by a boy of about ten, who moved up to stand by her side. The woman, just turned thirty, was tall, slim and good-looking with blonde hair and blue eyes. The boy was a sturdy youngster with the same colour hair as his mother.

As the woman looked up at him Jack got the impression that she was in some kind of trouble. Her eyes were swollen as if she had been weeping, and she looked distressed. He tipped the brim of his hat.

'Howdy, ma'am,' he said. 'I'd be obliged if you'd tell me where I'll find the nearest town.'

'The place you want is Monroe,' she said, taking a close look at Jack, and noticing that he wasn't wearing a gun and that there was a certain lack of animation in his bearing. 'Ride another four miles down the valley, past the other five homesteads that are strung along the river. Then head south and leave the valley through a narrow gap in the ridge. Follow the trail and you'll find Monroe about one mile ahead.'

'I'm obliged, ma'am,' said Jack, and started turning his mount to leave. He paused as she spoke again. There was a note of desperation in her voice.

'I was wondering,' she said, 'if you're looking for work. Me and young Danny here ain't quite up to running this place on our own. We need a man's help. I'll pay the going wage for the job, and a little over.'

Jack avoided the woman's gaze.

'I'm sorry, ma'am,' he said. 'I don't reckon I'd be much use to you.'

He turned his horse and rode back towards the trail which ran along the homestead. The woman, head bowed, put an arm around her son's shoulders and they both went back into the house.

Just before he reached the trail Jack halted and pondered for a while. He was beginning to realize that for some time he had done little more than wallow in his own misery, and that maybe the time had come for him to snap out of his present condition and start doing something useful for a change.

He turned his horse and rode back towards the house. The woman, who had been watching him through the window, came out again with the boy. Jack stopped in front of them.

'That job,' said Jack. 'I'll take it if the offer's still open.'

'It's yours,' she said. He could see the relief on her face. 'You done any farming before?'

'For a few years,' replied Jack, 'I helped my folks run a homestead in Kansas.'

'I'm Miriam Farrell,' she said, 'and this is Danny.'

'Jack Nelson,' said Jack.

'There's a bunk in the barn you can use,' she said. 'Danny'll show you where it is. I'll take some blankets out there later. Supper'll be ready in an hour. Have a look round the place before then if you like.'

She went back inside the house and the boy took Jack over to the barn and showed him the bunk standing in a corner at the back. Jack took the saddle and bridle off his horse and accompanied by Danny he led his mount to the pasture.

Then with the boy by his side, he had a look around the homestead. There was a field of corn and one of potatoes, both looking in reasonable shape.

'Pa was figuring on buying a few steers soon,' said Danny, 'and growing some hay for winter feed.'

'Something happened to your pa?' asked Jack.

The boy was obviously upset.

'Pa fell off his horse,' he said, 'on the way into town. He was killed. He ain't never coming back.'

They both went back to the house for supper.

As he sat at the table it was clear to Jack that Miriam Farrell was an excellent cook, and he put away a meal the like of which he had not enjoyed for a long time. She and the boy said little during the meal, but when she had cleared up after it, and had sent Danny to bed, she sat down to talk to Jack.

'Before you decide to stay on,' she said, 'it's only fair to tell you that Willard Duff ain't going to like you helping me out. He's the owner of the Box D Ranch and his range covers most of the valley. He's a big, overbearing man. His ranch house is close by the river, further down the valley.

'He's let it be known around here that he ain't in favour of anybody working for me. That's why I ain't been able to hire anybody before. I can't blame you if you change your mind.'

'What does this Duff have against you?' asked Jack.

'I'm pretty sure he wants me out,' she replied. 'He's a greedy man, and you can see how the homestead is blocking part of his range from the water.

'He called in a couple of weeks ago to make me an offer to quit the place, but I turned him down flat. Even if I wanted to leave, which I don't, where would we go? I have no kin left alive.'

'I've been drifting a long time,' said Jack, 'with nothing to show for it. It's just hit me that it's time I was doing something useful again. I figure you've done me a good turn, offering me this job. I reckon I'll stay on.'

'Thanks,' she said. 'I guess you're wondering how Danny and me come to be alone like this?'

'Danny told me his father had an accident,' said Jack.

'That's right,' she said. 'It was five weeks ago. Clem set off for town on horseback after breakfast. Outside the valley the trail into town passes near the top of a gorge for a spell. A rider from the Box D who was riding into town around noon saw Clem's horse standing there. Then he spotted a body lying at the bottom of the gorge.

'It was Clem down there, with bad injuries to his head and body. He was dead. Clem was a very careful man and a good rider, and I just couldn't figure out how it happened that he was riding so close to the gorge and got thrown into it. It's a question that still worries me.'

'You figure that maybe it wasn't an accident?' asked Jack.

'There's nothing to prove that,' she replied, 'but I can't get the thought out of my mind. Duff had been pestering Clem to quit for several weeks before he died.'

TWO

Jack soon settled down to work on the homestead and his depression started to lift. He had willing helpers in Danny and his mother, and the slight signs of neglect which he had noticed when he first rode in disappeared after a few days.

He was working in the potato field one day with Danny when they saw a rider approach the house and dismount. He stood looking at them for a while.

'That's Brad Duff,' said Danny. 'He's Willard Duff's son.'

They watched as Miriam Farrell came out of the house and talked for a while with Duff. Then she turned abruptly and went back inside. Duff shouted something after her, then turned to look at Jack and Danny again. Then he mounted and rode off.

Shortly after this Jack and Danny went in for a meal. Danny's mother looked angry. Her face was flushed.

'I've just had another offer if I quit the place,' she said. 'It's a better offer than before, but I told Brad Duff I just wasn't interested.

'He asked me who the man was working in the field. I told him it was somebody I'd hired, and as to who it was, that was none of his business.

'Then he got me pretty riled. He said that the best solution would be for me to marry him and go and live with him and his father at the ranch house. I told him the idea made me feel sick, then I went back into the house. He shouted after me that he'd be round again before long.'

'The more I hear about the Duffs, the less I like the sound of them,' said Jack. 'Has Willard Duff offered anything to any of the other homesteaders to quit?'

'Not yet,' she replied. 'The other settlers all looked on Clem as somebody they could turn to for advice. Maybe Duff thought that if he could get Clem to move, it would be easier for him to get the others to follow.'

The following day, two neighbouring settlers, Grant and Dixon, called in to see Miriam Farrell. She was sure that the news had got around about her new hand, and that it was mainly curiosity that had brought them there.

Grant, a big strong man well over six feet tall, had the quarter section next to hers. He and his wife had moved out west from Illinois with their young son Joey. He had given Miriam help, from time to time, after her husband died, but now he was fully occupied on his own land.

Dixon, who was working the claim on the other side of Grant's, was a man of average height, thin and wiry, who hailed from Indiana. He had brought a wife with him, but no children.

Miriam Farrell introduced the two men to Jack and he could sense that he was under close scrutiny. After chatting for a while about farming in general, the two visitors left.

Two days later Jack drove the buckboard into Monroe for supplies. Miriam Farrell and Danny accompanied him. On the way they stopped near the place where Clem Farrell had fallen to his death, and Jack climbed out and walked over to look down into the gorge.

When they reached Monroe they stopped outside the store and Danny and his mother went inside. Jack stood beside the buckboard and looked along the street. There was little movement on it, but he noticed three horses standing outside the saloon next door.

Inside the store, Miriam found Will Ranger, the storekeeper, and his wife Emily, who had been close friends of the Farrells for some time. Miriam gave her list of supplies to Will Ranger, then Emily drew her aside as Danny left the store to rejoin Jack.

'I hear you've hired a hand, Miriam,' she said.

'That's right,' said Miriam. 'He's outside. I was lucky. A stranger rode in for directions and I offered him work. So far, I'm mightily pleased with the way he's doing the job.'

'D'you know anything about him?' asked Emily.

'No, I don't,' replied Miriam. 'He ain't exactly a talkative man. But he knows about farming and I feel easy with him around.'

'I'm glad you got yourself a hand, Miriam,' said Emily, 'but I've got to warn you. You know what a narrow-minded lot they are around here. Folks are talking about you and the hand living out there alone, except for Danny.'

'I ain't got much choice,' said Miriam. 'Folks can think what they like.'

Outside, Danny and Jack were both standing by the buckboard when three men came out of the saloon.

'Those three are hands from the Box D,' said Danny. 'I've seen them in town before. The big one's called Martin.'

Martin looked over at Jack and Danny,

then spoke to his two companions. All three of them looked at the man and the boy by the buckboard and one of them said something which seemed to amuse the others. Grinning, they all stepped off the boardwalk and walked along the street towards the buckboard.

Martin, who was slightly in the lead, was a big, strong-looking man, quarrelsome by nature, who topped Jack by a couple of inches. His companions were called Jackson and Miller. All three were carrying side-arms. Still grinning, they stopped in front of Jack and the boy. They eyed Jack for a few moments before Martin spoke.

'I figure you're the hand working out at the Farrell place,' he said, noting that Jack was not wearing a gun.

'That's right,' said Jack, quietly.

'Mr Duff don't want a stranger working out there,' said Martin. 'It ain't going to be healthy for you to stay on at the homestead. Your best plan would be to move out of the valley.'

'It don't bother me none what Duff wants,' said Jack, evenly. 'Mrs Farrell's the only one who can tell me what to do. Tell Duff not to stick his nose into other people's affairs.'

Martin flushed with anger, rather taken aback by Jack's attitude.

'It don't seem decent,' he said, with a sneer, 'the Farrell woman taking up with another man, and her husband hardly settled in his grave.'

'I thought, when I first laid eyes on you, Martin,' said Jack, 'that you had the look of a bully about you. Now I can see I was right. And a foul-mouthed bully at that.'

He turned to Danny.

'Just step up on the boardwalk, will you, Danny?' he said.

Danny hesitated, then ran around the buckboard and jumped up on to the board-walk. He turned to look at Jack and the three men confronting him. Grant, the home-steader, who had just ridden up to the store, dismounted and joined the boy. A moment later, Miriam Farrell came out of the store and walked up to her son. The storekeeper, Will Ranger, came out behind her.

Martin, incensed, glared at Jack, who had moved further out into the street. He decided to teach him a lesson. He was well known among the Box D hands as a man who relished the task of beating the senses out of an opponent, and that's just what he was aiming to do to Jack. A few passers-by, sensing that a fight was in the offing, moved up to watch the spectacle.

Martin advanced to within a few feet of Jack, then he paused.

'After the beating I'm going to give you,' he said, 'you'll be sorry you ever met up with me.' His voice was harsh with rage.

Jack stood motionless, his face impassive, his body seemingly relaxed, until Martin launched himself on his opponent in a wild rush, his right fist raised to smash against Jack's head.

Jack glided smoothly to one side and diverted the blow with his forearm. Martin blundered past him for a few feet before he could stop. Then he turned, cursed, and launched himself at Jack once again.

This time, Jack grabbed Martin's right wrist in his own right hand, ran backwards several paces, pulling Martin with him, then suddenly wheeled around and pushed his right hip backwards, against his opponent. He gave a mighty heave on Martin's arm, and using his opponent's momentum to assist the manoeuvre, he threw the Box D hand over his shoulder.

Martin flew through the air and landed heavily on his back on the ground, with the wind knocked out of him. Jack stood waiting until his opponent had recovered sufficiently to rise to his feet.

'You had enough?' he asked.

Martin was not without courage. He snorted and came at Jack once again, watching for any unconventional move on his opponent's part. But this time Jack stood his ground, easily dodged the blow which Martin aimed at his head, and delivered two body blows so powerful that Martin staggered backwards and dropped his hands.

Jack followed up, and in quick succession he delivered two solid right-hand punches to the side of Martin's jaw. The Box D hand fell to the ground and lay motionless.

Jack, only slightly out of breath, looked across at Jackson and Miller, neither of whom was a match for Martin in a fist-fight. They were both staring incredulously at the man lying on the ground. It was the first time they had ever seen their companion vanquished in a hand-to-hand fight.

'You men want to take up where Martin left off?' Jack enquired.

The two men hesitated, then shook their heads.

'Better see to your friend then,' said Jack.

Miller and Jackson walked up to Martin, who was stirring. They helped him up, then over to the horses outside the saloon. He sat on the boardwalk for a short while, then painfully mounted his horse and rode out of town with his two companions.

Jack went back to wait by the buckboard, and the small group of onlookers dispersed. Grant stepped off the boardwalk and walked up to Jack. Danny and his mother were close behind him.

'What was that all about?' asked Grant.

'That Box D man,' replied Jack, 'didn't like the idea of me working on the homestead. So I had to make it clear to him that I ain't going to leave.'

'Are you sure about staying?' asked Miriam Farrell. 'Duff's a powerful man and he ain't going to be pleased about what you just did to Martin.'

'It's just that I don't like being told what to do,' said Jack. 'I've always been like that. Besides, I like working on the homestead.'

'All right,' she said, 'but I've got a feeling we haven't heard the last of Duff.'

'It's puzzled the rest of us settlers,' said Grant, 'that none of us has been bothered by Duff so far.'

'My guess is,' said Jack, 'that things ain't going to stay like that. I reckon you and the others should watch out for trouble.'

After they had loaded the supplies on to the buckboard, Jack and the Farrells left Grant, now a worried man, and headed for the homestead. In the evening, after Danny had gone to bed, Miriam Farrell told Jack that she had learnt from her son what Martin had said about her.

'I'm obliged to you,' she said, 'for giving the man a beating after what he said, but I still think you'd be wise to leave. You're going to be in a lot of danger if you stay here.'

'It's me that's obliged to you,' said Jack, 'for giving me something worthwhile to do. I've been drifting too long. I aim to stay on here and find out just what Duff's up to.'

Over the next two weeks they saw an occasional Box D hand riding the range, but none of them came on to the homestead. The only visitors were the three settlers that Jack hadn't met up to then. He figured that they were curious about him.

They came at different times, chatted for a

while, then left. Counting eastwards along the valley, they were Fisher, Randle and Lee. All were married. Randle and Lee both had a young son and daughter, and hailed from Indiana. Fisher, in his fifties, and older than the others, had come from Illinois. He had no children. Jack sensed that they were all concerned about the possibility of confrontations with Duff.

The first sign of trouble came three weeks after Jack's encounter with Martin. During the course of one day, Willard Duff, accompanied by his son Brad and three hands, visited the five homesteads east of the Farrell quarter section.

At each homestead the rancher put exactly the same proposition. He said that he intended to bring more cattle into the valley, which meant that he needed the whole of the valley for his range, and the settlers would all have to quit. He was a reasonable man, he told them, and he was willing to pay each of them 600 dollars to leave their homesteads.

He gave them a week to make up their minds about accepting his offer and left with a veiled threat as to the consequences if they failed to do so. Night was falling as the rancher and his men rode away from the last homestead.

Later in the evening all the settlers who had been visited by the rancher and his men during the day rode up to the Farrell homestead just as Jack and the Farrells were finishing supper. Miriam Farrell invited them in and they all sat down.

'We're here,' said Grant, 'because of a visit we all had today from Willard Duff.'

He repeated what had been said at the meetings.

'The question we're all asking,' he said, 'is what are we going to do, seeing as there's no lawman around here we can turn to? I told the others how Nelson here tamed Martin of the Box D in town today, and we thought that maybe he could give us some advice about what we should do.'

'What's happening here,' said Jack, 'is

happening in a lot of other places. Trouble is, the law's spread too thin and it's going to be a while before that's put right. Meanwhile, a lot of settlers who're being threatened are having to decide whether to face up to the big ranchers or quit. It's something each settler has got to decide for himself.'

'What about you?' asked Dixon.

'That's up to Mrs Farrell,' Jack replied. 'If she decides to stay on I'll do the same.'

'I'm not quitting,' said Miriam Farrell. 'We have the legal right to stay on our quarter sections.'

After some discussion, during which Jack learnt that all the men working the other homesteads had served as soldiers in the Union Army during the Civil War, it was decided that none of them would accept the rancher's offer.

Before they left, Jack warned them that Duff might try to scare them into leaving. If Duff started on that tack, Jack told them of a plan he had in mind for dealing with the situation.

THREE

Four days after the visit of Willard Duff to the homesteads Jack took a canvas sack out of the barn and dropped it in the buckboard. Then he drove the buckboard into town for some supplies. Danny accompanied him. He was lively and intelligent and Jack had taken quite a liking to him.

'You like farming, Danny?' he asked the boy.

'I think so,' said Danny, 'but I'd like to travel around the country a bit first, to see all the places I've heard about.'

When they reached Monroe, Jack drove the buckboard up to the store and he and Danny went inside. Will Ranger was behind the counter. He introduced Jack to a customer, Doc Shannon, who was just leaving. Shannon was a pleasant looking, middle-aged man who lived in town. After a short conversation the doctor left and Jack gave Ranger a list of supplies. The storekeeper started stacking them against the counter.

'They're still talking in town about how you cut Martin down to size,' he told Jack. 'He was a bully, always looking for a quarrel, and mighty unpopular around here. You'd better watch out. I reckon he'll be looking for revenge.'

Lifting an item off one of the shelves, he glanced out of the window and stiffened.

'And the time to watch out is right now,' he said. 'Brad Duff is just riding into town with Martin.'

Jack walked over to the window and looked out. The two men were dismounting outside the saloon. Brad Duff, who he had already seen at a distance when the rancher's son visited the homestead, was a big man, a little overweight, with hard eyes, a thick moustache, and an arrogant look about him. Each of the two men was wearing a sidearm.

'It might be a good idea,' said Ranger, 'if you ride out of town while those two are still in the saloon. I've heard that Brad Duff has a pretty high opinion of himself as a gun-fighter. Likes to practise his shooting. And fair play don't mean anything to him. Maybe he wouldn't take too much notice of the fact that you ain't wearing a gun.'

As they watched the two men entered the saloon and disappeared from view. Jack went out to the buckboard and picked up the sack he had placed in it earlier.

He took the sack into the store, lifted out the gunbelt and holstered gun from inside it, and buckled the belt on. He lifted the Colt .45 Peacemaker from the holster, checked it, and replaced it. The way he handled the gun as Danny and Ranger watched him indicated a familiarity with the weapon which impressed the storekeeper.

'Just in case,' said Jack to Ranger. 'I ain't looking for no trouble.'

Ranger nodded and continued collecting the items on the shopping list.

'How many hands are there on the Box D?' asked Jack.

'About fourteen in all, I reckon,' Ranger replied, 'and a tough looking bunch they are. Brad Duff is the ramrod.'

Five minutes later the door opened and Martin walked into the store. His face still showed signs of his recent encounter with Jack. He stopped short as he saw Jack and noted that he was armed. Jack waved him up to the counter where he bought some tobacco, then left. Looking through the window, Jack saw him hurry over to the saloon and go inside.

Ten minutes later the supplies were ready, and Jack and Ranger carried them out to the buckboard. Just as they completed the loading, the saloon doors swung open and Brad Duff and his companion came out on to the boardwalk and stood looking at Jack along the street, near the back of the buckboard.

Jack glanced at them, then spoke to Ranger.

'I reckon the best place for you and Danny

just now is inside the store,' he suggested.

Ranger nodded and hastily ushered Danny into the store. Once inside they both stood at the window, looking out on to the street.

'Is he going to be all right, Mr Ranger?' asked Danny.

'I sure hope so, Danny,' replied the storekeeper. 'I've got a feeling he is.'

Along the street the two men stepped down off the boardwalk and approached Jack, with Brad Duff slightly in the lead.

Jack turned to face them as they halted and stood, side by side, a few yards away from him.

'I've been wanting to meet you, Nelson,' said Duff, 'and seeing you here saves me from coming out to the homestead. We don't want you here in the valley unsettling the homesteaders and beating up Box D hands.

'I'm giving you the chance to leave today without you getting yourself hurt. We'll ride back to the homestead with you and you can pick up your things there. Then we'll see

39

you out of the valley. And if you show your face here again you'll be shot on sight.'

'But I like it here,' said Jack. 'It's good farming land and I've got a good job. I just don't feel like moving on whatever you say.'

Brad Duff's face hardened.

'There ain't no point in your staying on here,' he said. 'If the settlers ain't out of the valley three days from now we'll run them out and likely some of them'll get hurt.'

'That's one reason I'm staying on,' said Jack. 'I aim to help them to hang on to their homesteads.'

Brad Duff sneered. 'It looks to me,' he said, 'like the gossip about you and the Farrell woman is true.'

'And it looks to me like you're just as foulmouthed as Martin here,' said Jack. 'I've heard that you fancy yourself as a gunfighter and I've got a feeling that you're just itching to pull that gun of yours.

'But you'd be making a big mistake, Duff. Before either of you pulled the trigger, you'd have collected my first bullet. And likely, I'd be able to plug Martin as well. So I recommend that you stop hassling me and ride back to the ranch.'

The two men stared at Jack. He had spoken quietly, but there was something about his stance, the set of his face and the look in his eye which sent a sudden chill through them. Duff's hand inched towards his six-shooter, then stopped short. Martin stood motionless.

Then Duff's confidence in his own gun-handling ability returned. He reached for his revolver and made a draw which was well up to his usual standard. Jack started his move at the same time and to the onlookers, including Ranger and Danny inside the store, the Peacemaker seemed to appear miraculously in his right hand and was lined up, cocked and fired before Duff was ready to trigger his gun.

The bullet struck Duff in the right shoulder and he dropped his gun and staggered back a few paces. Martin, belatedly going for his gun, froze as he looked into the unwavering muzzle of Jack's cocked pistol, pointed at his forehead.

Jack plucked Martin's gun from its holster and picked Duff's six-shooter off the ground. Then he spoke to Duff.

'I told you not to try it, Duff,' he said. 'You're lucky I wasn't aiming to kill you. When the doc's had a look at that shoulder you two had better ride out of town. Meanwhile, I'll hang on to these two guns just in case you're fool enough to try to use them on me again.'

Duff glared at him.

'You're going to be sorry you ever fired that shot,' he said. His voice was harsh with pain and rage.

'Get moving!' said Jack, and watched as Martin collected the two horses and led them along the street towards the doctor's house, with Duff walking slowly by his side, holding his injured shoulder.

When they had disappeared into the doctor's house, Jack stepped on to the boardwalk to join Ranger and Danny, who had come out of the store.

'You sure taught them two a lesson,' said Ranger, 'but what happens now?'

'I guess we can expect trouble out at the homesteads when the deadline expires three days from now,' Jack replied. 'We'll head back there right now. I need to talk with the settlers.'

When they reached the Farrell homestead, Jack told Miriam about his encounter with Brad Duff and Martin. Then he rode to the other homesteads and asked the men to meet at the Farrell homestead so that they could all discuss the situation together. He told them about the incident in town and about Duff's threat to run them all out of the valley, by force if necessary, if they were still there in three days' time.

When they were all assembled there later in the day, Jack told them that if they wanted to hear them he had some ideas about how they might deal with the situation. He said he was certain they were going to be in serious danger when the deadline had passed.

'I'd sure like to hear those ideas myself,' said Miriam. 'It ain't easy to see how we're going to get out of the fix we're in.'

The others nodded assent.

'Maybe I should tell you,' said Jack, 'that I've served as a deputy sheriff, then as a sheriff, in Kansas, so I've had plenty of dealings with people who think they're above the law. The first thing to do is get the women and children out of the valley, so that we can deal with Duff without having to worry about them all the time. When we've moved them out we can decide how to deal with Duff and his men.'

The settlers looked taken aback by the idea.

'But where would they go?' asked Randle.

'On my way here,' said Jack, 'I stayed for a while with a prospector called Hiram Benson in a ravine about fifteen miles west of here. It's a sheltered spot, with plenty of water, and no main trails nearby. And it's well away from the valley. They should be pretty safe there for a while.

'The prospector might still be there, living in the old shack he found in the ravine. But even if he's gone, and the shack's not in use, it's not big enough for everybody. I spotted some small surplus Army tents in the store in Monroe, which Ranger said he'd been trying to sell for quite a while. Maybe they'd be useful to give your families some shelter in the ravine.'

'I've got to say,' said Grant, 'that I favour the idea of getting my family out of harm's way while we face up to Duff. I may have a hard job persuading Ethel, but in the end I think she'll see that it's the best thing to do.'

Miriam and the men discussed the matter at length and decided to go ahead with Jack's plan.

'I don't like it,' said Miriam, 'but I can see it's best for all of us if the women and children quit the valley for a while. When do we leave?'

'Just after dark tomorrow would be a good time,' Jack replied. 'We don't want anybody from the Box D to see you go. I'll lead you there.

'And during the day a couple of buckboards had better be driven into town to pick up the tents and enough supplies to last for a month or so in the ravine. If we ask Ranger, I'm sure he'll keep quiet about the load they're carrying.

'I reckon three buckboards should be enough to take everybody out there. That leaves three for us to use in the valley. There's no need for any of the men except myself to go along. If I leave the buckboards there, and lead the horses back, I should get back around daylight, and it ain't likely I'll be spotted by anybody from the Box D.'

During the following morning Jack rode along the trail running eastward past the homesteads. He continued until he spotted the Box D ranch buildings in the distance. Three hundred yards ahead of him he could see the fork which branched off and ran southward to Monroe. He paused for a while, looking round him, then returned to the homestead.

By sundown the three buckboards, assembled at the Farrell homestead, were ready to leave. The men said their goodbyes and Jack, driving the first buckboard, headed west up the valley. The other two buckboards were driven by the wives of Fisher and Randle.

Helped by an almost full moon they made good time, and there were still a few hours left before dawn when Jack halted just outside the ravine, with the other two buckboards close behind him. He climbed down and told the others that he was going to walk up the ravine to see whether Benson was still there.

He entered the mouth of the ravine and walked silently towards the shack. Halfway there he saw a picketed mule and burro. They looked like the animals Benson had been using when Jack first met him. He walked up to the shack and banged on the door.

'It's Jack Nelson,' he called. 'You in there,

Hiram?' As he shouted his name again, he heard the sounds of movement inside the shack. The door partly opened and Benson, holding his shotgun, peered out.

'It's Jack Nelson,' said Jack, and lit a match to show his face.

'Jack!' said Benson. 'What in tarnation are you doing here in the middle of the night?'

He opened the door to let Jack in and lit a lamp.

Jack briefly explained the situation, telling Benson that the women and children were waiting outside the ravine.

'This is a good place to hide,' said the prospector. 'I ain't seen a soul since you left. Bring 'em in while I get dressed and put some wood on the stove. I could do with some company for a while. Since you left I've noticed I've been talking to myself a lot. It can't be healthy.'

Jack walked back to the others.

'Benson's still there,' he told them, 'and really looking forward to your company. Let's go.'

He drove his buckboard up to the shack. The others followed him. Benson was waiting at the door. Jack and the six women and six children all climbed down from the buckboards and assembled in front of the prospector.

'I sure am glad to see you folks,' he said. 'Like I told Jack here, I gets a mite lonely at times. Come right in. It's going to be crowded, but as soon as it's daylight we'll get those tents up so's you'll have a bit more room. Meantime, the stove's burning and you can have a hot drink if that's what anybody would like.'

Jack left half an hour later after suggesting that, day and night, in order to be on the safe side, they should station a lookout with a rifle. He was riding one of the horses which had pulled the buckboards, and was leading the rest. Before leaving he promised that the women would be kept advised, whenever it was possible, of the progress of the confrontation with Duff and his men.

When he reached the Farrell homestead

just after dawn, the settlers were waiting there for him, ready to discuss the plan of campaign.

'Any time after the deadline has passed,' said Jack, 'when Duff knows that nobody is quitting, he'll be bent on forcing us out. So we've got to be ready for trouble, and that means that everybody needs to wear a gun all the time and keep a rifle in a saddle holster when riding. It's a good thing all you men have army experience.

'During the day we need to have a lookout, with field-glasses, on top of that knoll just outside Mr Dixon's place. From there he should be able to see riders heading this way when they're still a long way off. The rest of us can carry on with the work on the homesteads.

'If the lookout spots Box D riders heading our way he'll fire off three shots to alert the rest of us and we'll all join up outside the Lee homestead, that being the one nearest to the Box D ranch building. We'll face the Box D men together when they turn up, and if you like, I'll do the talking. I don't think they'd want to risk a shoot-out in daylight with a bunch of six armed men.'

'That seems like a good plan,' said Grant, 'but what about the nights? That's when they're most likely to hit us.'

'You're right,' said Jack. 'I think we'd better all stay at Mr Lee's place during the night. And we'll need two lookouts. The rest of us can sleep.'

'Two lookouts?' queried Lee. 'Where'll they be stationed?'

'One'll be in the loft in your barn,' Jack replied. 'As for the other, I noticed when I rode along the trail the other day towards the Box D ranch house, that just before it meets the trail coming from Monroe, it runs through a narrow gap between two groves of trees, and on one side of this gap is a rock outcrop about thirty feet high, which can be seen from your place.

'I reckon the other lookout should be on top of that outcrop, with one of the big lamps we use in the barns. If he sees a bunch of riders pass who are heading for the homesteads, he'll light the lamp and hold it so's the lookout in the loft of your barn can see it. I noticed that the outcrop can be seen from that opening in the wall of the loft.'

'And what happens when they get here?' asked Lee.

'Today,' replied Jack, 'at the south-east corner of your homestead, near to the trail, we'll dig a trench big enough for three of us to stand in with our rifles. Then we'll dig another trench, to take two of us, outside the homestead, on the other side of the trail.

'We'll go to the trenches during the night if we get the signal from the lookout. Shooting at them from cover in the dark like we'll be doing, and from both sides, I reckon our gunfire'll be enough to turn the Box D men back, even if we fire over their heads. There's no cover for them to use. So I figure that's what we should do.

'We'll stay in the trenches till we're sure they've gone. And we'll make sure the trenches are safely covered over in the daytime. How does the plan strike you all?'

During the following discussion nobody could think of a better plan and it was agreed that lookouts would be stationed, starting the following morning. Then they all went out to dig the trenches.

FOUR

The following day, only one Box D rider was sighted. He was riding alone along the valley, well away from the homesteads. And during the following night there was no sign of approaching riders.

But the day after that, a group of ten men, led by Willard Duff himself, was spotted by the lookout, Dixon. They were riding towards the homesteads. Dixon scrambled down from the knoll and fired warning shots to alert Jack and the other settlers, who quickly armed themselves and joined Dixon at the Lee homestead.

They all stood on the trail outside the homestead, holding their rifles and awaiting the arrival of Duff and his men. Jack stood slightly in front of the others.

The Box D riders, with Duff in the lead,

54

slowed down to a walk as they approached the group of six men blocking the trail in front of them. They stopped a few yards away from the settlers.

It was the first time Jack had seen the rancher. Like his son he was a big man, slightly overweight, with the same cruel and arrogant look about him. He was wearing a goatee beard. Scowling, he looked at Jack.

'I expect you're Nelson,' he said. His voice was harsh and threatening.

'That's right,' said Jack.

'All these settlers,' said Duff, 'were told that if they didn't accept my offer for them to quit their homesteads, I would have to move them out by force. That's why we're here now. I'd advise them all to leave quietly. And that goes for you too, Nelson. All my men are pretty good at handling a gun, so if you're thinking of making a fight of it, I can tell you, you wouldn't stand a chance.'

'Don't you be too sure about that,' said Jack. 'Every one of these homesteaders served in the Union Army. And there's another thing. I am one hundred per cent sure, just like I was with your son, that I could plug you before I go down myself. So I think your best plan would be to turn round and ride out of here before you get killed.'

Duff's face reddened. Closely observed by Jack, he rested his hand on his gun handle and opened his mouth to order his men to fire. Then, remembering what his son had told him of Jack's gun-handling expertise, and sensing that the man in front of him was ready to explode into swift and violent action, he reluctantly changed his mind. He didn't mind a few of his men going down, but it was a different matter when his own life was at stake.

Fuming, he spoke to Jack.

'This ain't the end of this, Nelson,' he said. 'You're going to be sorry you took the side of these settlers.'

'Whatever you do, Duff,' said Jack, 'we'll be ready for you. Keep away from the homesteads.'

Abruptly, Duff wheeled his horse and rode back along the trail. His men followed suit.

Jack and the others watched until the rancher and his men were out of sight. Then Grant spoke to Jack.

'Lucky you were here, I reckon,' he said, 'otherwise they might have taken us on. What d'you reckon Duff's going to do next?'

'My guess is,' replied Jack, 'that maybe his men'll pay us a visit during the night. We'll have to be ready for them.'

The men all returned to their quarter sections, except Grant, who took his turn as lookout on the knoll. After dark, they all assembled at Lee's homestead and May rode off to the lookout point on the outcrop for the overnight watch, while Jack took the first watch at the homestead. Fisher replaced him at midnight.

It was around two in the morning when May heard a group of riders approaching from the east. Looking down on to the trail, he could see the shapes of about ten mounted men below.

He waited until they had passed, then quickly lit the big oil lamp he had brought with him. Facing the homesteads, he waved it from side to side. Fisher, on lookout in the loft of Lee's barn, saw the distant light and hurried to alert Jack and the others.

Carrying their rifles, they ran to the trenches, two to one, three to the other, and jumped down into them. The settlers had been told by Jack not to aim to kill. He told them to fire just over the heads of the oncoming riders when they drew close.

It was not long before they heard the sounds of the approaching horses, and as soon as they could see the dim outlines of the animals and their riders through the darkness, they set up a rapid continuous fire from both sides which took the Box D men entirely by surprise.

They reined in their startled mounts abruptly, wheeled them, and with no inclination to stay and return the fire from such an exposed position, they raced back along the trail.

Jack and the others waited for half an hour in the trenches, but there was no sign of the riders returning. Leaving a lookout on duty again, the others, except Jack, went to their beds. He had decided to follow the departing riders at a distance.

He went warily, in case they had halted somewhere along the trail, but saw no sign of them. He rode past the outcrop, knowing that May was perched on top, and continued on until the Box D ranch buildings loomed up out of the darkness.

He stopped, and as he watched, he saw lights go out, first in the house, then, shortly after, in a building which he guessed to be the bunkhouse. No other lights were showing.

He dismounted and tied his horse to the rail of the nearby corral. Then he waited half an hour before moving stealthily to examine the layout of the buildings and the outside of each building. Coming to the barn, he also went inside and struck a few matches to check the contents.

He did the same thing when he came to two small sheds standing near the barn. Then he went on to take a look at the windmill standing close to the river. When he finally left he felt confident that he had found out as much as possible about the place.

He stopped when he reached the outcrop where May was stationed, and shouted up to him.

'This is Nelson,' he called. 'You can come back to the homestead with me. You'll see no more Box D men tonight.'

Getting no reply, he repeated the message, and this time May answered and said he was coming down. He appeared a few minutes later with his horse and they rode back to the Lee homestead together.

Later, over breakfast, Jack and the others discussed the situation.

'What d'you think Duff's liable to do now?' Dixon asked Jack.

'What he'd probably hoped to do,' said

Jack, 'was to pick you off one at a time. But now that we're all facing him together he knows he can't do that. So he'll have to think up some other plan. He's probably working on that now and maybe it'll be a little while before he moves in on us again.

'But I don't think we should wait until that time comes. I think we should do some hell-raising ourselves. My guess is that the last thing he's expecting is for *us* to move against *him*.'

'I guess you're right,' said Randle, 'and I'm game, but only because my wife and children are safe away from here. That was a good idea of yours, sending them to that ravine. What sort of hell-raising d'you have in mind?'

Jack explained his plan for taking the fight to Duff.

'I ain't so sure we should do that,' said Lee. 'Maybe after he's seen that we're not going to give in without a fight, Duff'll give up on the idea of forcing us out.'

'Myself, I can't see him doing that,' said

Jack. 'I don't think we've done enough yet to make him think seriously about leaving you alone. But you've got to make the choice yourselves. Maybe you should vote on it.'

They decided to do this and the result was that three of the five, Lee, Randle and Fisher, voted in favour of waiting to see if Duff had abandoned his plans to move them out.

Over the next two days and nights they kept lookouts in the same positions as before, but there was no sign of any attack by men from the Box D.

On the third day after they had taken the vote, Lee was ploughing a field adjacent to the river on his homestead. As he reached the end of a furrow he paused to mop his brow and rest for a few moments. He was just about to resume when he suddenly jerked backwards as a rifle bullet penetrated the upper part of his body. A moment later the sound of a rifle shot came from the other side of the river.

Randle and Fisher, working on the next

two homesteads up the river, heard the single shot and rode along to the Lee homestead to investigate. They found Lee lying on the ground, badly wounded in the chest, but still alive. They saw no sign of the rifleman who had shot him down.

They carried him into the house and laid him on the bed.

'I'm riding into town for Doc Shannon,' said Randle to Fisher. 'See if you can stop the bleeding. With luck, I'll be back within the hour.'

As Randle left, Fisher started to make up a pad, and when it was ready he placed it over the wound. Lee was still conscious, but obviously very weak and in pain.

When Randle returned with the doctor, Fisher rode off to tell Jack and the other homesteaders what had happened. They all rode back to the Lee homestead. When Jack arrived the doctor was fixing a bandage around Lee's chest after digging out the rifle bullet which had struck him.

He told Jack and the others that the bullet

had missed the heart and other vital organs, and if infection didn't get to be a problem there was a good chance that Lee would survive, with proper rest and care. He said he would come out daily to see how the patient was progressing.

Jack explained the absence of Lee's family to the doctor and told him that the families of the other settlers had also moved out of harm's way. He asked the doctor not to mention their absence in town.

Shannon offered to look after Lee at his house in Monroe as soon as the settler was fit to travel.

'That'd be a big help to us,' said Jack.

'I'm offering to do it,' said the doctor, 'because I don't agree with the way that Duff completely ignores the law. And I ain't the only one in town that thinks that way.'

When the doctor had gone Lee told Jack that he was facing the river when shot, and although he had seen no one he was sure that the man with the rifle must have been somewhere on the far side.

'I'm going over there now,' said Jack, 'to have a look round.'

He rode west up the valley till he came to a fording point where he could cross the river. Then he rode back along the bank until he was opposite the Lee homestead. Riding slowly back and forth along the river bank, he made a close search of the ground stretching back a little way from the river. Then he rode back to rejoin the others at the Lee homestead.

He told them that the man who had fired the shot had been alone and had hidden in a patch of brush on the far side of the river. Earlier, he had left his horse in a small copse upstream and had half-run, half-crawled, to the brush. After the shooting he had returned to his horse in the same way and had ridden off to the east.

'I didn't see the man who did the shooting,' said Dixon, who had been on lookout on the knoll when it took place, and who had seen Randle and Fisher riding to investigate.

'Don't blame yourself,' said Jack. 'I could see that the man who fired that shot was an expert in keeping himself out of sight.'

Jack sat down with the settlers to discuss the implications of the shooting. Randle and Fisher, who had previously voted not to make any immediate move against Duff, said that they had now changed their minds and agreed with Jack's plan for taking the fight to the rancher. Mort Lee also was in favour of this move.

'I can see now,' said Randle, 'that we've to stop Duff somehow. He's stronger than we are, but all the same we've got to try. It's just a matter of luck that Mort ain't dead.'

'Right,' said Jack. 'We've got one thing in our favour. We'll have the advantage of surprise. I reckon Duff's so sure of himself that the idea of *us* moving against *him* would never enter his mind. But let's wait till Mort's safe at the doctor's place in town before we make our next move. Meanwhile, we'd better keep a sharp lookout for bushwhackers.'

Shannon rode out the following day and said that he was satisfied with Lee's progress.

During the following night Jack rode out to the ravine to tell the women about the situation on the homesteads. He called out to the woman standing guard in a cluster of rocks at the top of the wall at the ravine entrance. She was Ethel Grant. He rode on into the ravine, woke the women, and told them of recent events on the homestead. He assured Ruth Lee that the doctor reckoned her husband would make a full recovery.

Miriam Farrell spoke with him before he left.

'It's hard for us,' she said, 'hiding out here, wondering what's happening, and not being able to help.'

'I know that,' said Jack, 'but it gives us our best chance of getting the better of Duff. One of us'll ride out again before long to let you know how things are going.'

'We're wondering why it is,' she said, 'that you're staying on here to help us. It could be dangerous for you, and it's not as if you were a settler yourself.'

'I've been a lawman,' said Jack, 'and I can't rest easy when I can see somebody like Duff setting himself above the law. We've got to stop him somehow.'

During the afternoon after Jack's return to the homesteads, the doctor arrived in his buggy and took the wounded settler back with him to his house in Monroe.

FIVE

Darkness was falling as the doctor left and the two lookouts took up their posts. There were no alarms between then and midnight, at which time Jack and the three settlers at the homesteads assembled and rode off along the trail to the east. Each of them was carrying a large canvas sack, rolled up and tied on behind the saddle.

When they reached the outcrop from the top of which Dixon was watching the trail, they called up to him and a few minutes later he rode out from behind the outcrop and joined them.

Riding in silence, they headed for the Box D ranch buildings, and paused when these were just visible against the night sky. No lights were showing and there were no signs of activity. They rode up to the corral, which was between them and the buildings. They dismounted and tied their horses to the rails.

'I'll take a look around,' said Jack. 'Wait here till I get back.'

He disappeared into the darkness, to reappear fifteen minutes later, having circled the ranch house which stood close to the river, as well as all the other buildings.

'I was right,' he said, 'when I figured that Duff would never dream that anybody would have the gall to make a move against him right here on his own place. No guards have been posted and no lights are showing. We might as well get started. Take the sacks with you. You all know what to do. And remember, the last thing we want to do is wake somebody up.'

Jack and Grant, carrying two empty sacks, a sledgehammer and some rope, headed for the cook shack. Silently, they opened the door and entered, closing it behind them. The faint sound of the cook snoring came through the half-open door of a room tacked on to the end of the building.

Jack struck a match, took an oil lamp which was hanging from a peg on the wall, and lit it, leaving the wick well turned down. Holding the lamp he walked into the cook's bedroom and stood the lamp on a table. Grant followed him. The cook's snore was abruptly terminated when he was roughly turned over on to his front by Jack and felt the muzzle of a revolver jammed against the back of his neck.

'Stay quiet!' ordered Jack, 'and you won't get hurt.'

Quickly, Grant gagged and blindfolded the cook, then Jack trussed him so that he was barely able to move. Taking the lamp they left the room, closing the door behind them. Jack turned the lamp up and stood it on the big dining table.

He picked up the sledgehammer which he had left just inside the door and walked over to the big cast-iron stove. The fire inside it was out. He laid two towels along the top of the stove to deaden the sound of the impact, then struck the top three times with the sledgehammer. The cast-iron shattered under the heavy blows and the top of the stove, and part of the front, disintegrated. It was clear that in its present state it was unusable.

Jack went outside to confirm that the noise had disturbed nobody in the house or bunkhouse. There was no sign of light or movement in either. He went back into the cook shack and helped Grant to load into the sacks they had brought with them an assortment of pots, skillets, griddles and bread pans. Then, as silently as possible, they carried the sacks back to the horses.

While Jack and Grant were occupied in the cook shack, Dixon and Fisher went to one of the two sheds near to the barn, which had been pointed out to them by Jack as containing all the saddles, bridles and lariats used by Duff and his hands. They entered the shed, lit a lamp, and unstrapped the cinches from all the saddles. They dropped the cinches into the sacks, together with all the rope, lariats, head stalls, and bits that they could find. Then they carried the sacks over to the corral rails, where their horses were waiting.

Meanwhile, Randle had gone into the barn where, on his previous visit, Jack had seen that there was a big pile of winter hay for the saddle horses. He carried armfuls of this hay out to the tall windmill, which was being used to pump water from the river into a large tank close by its foot.

He piled heaps of hay around each of the four timber legs of the windmill, then soaked the hay and the bottoms of the legs with coal oil from the two big cans they had brought with them. Then he took one of the cans into the barn and sprinkled the oil liberally over the remaining pile of hay, so rendering most of it unsuitable for use as winter feed.

Going outside, Randle found Jack waiting for him and they ran over to the three settlers standing by the horses.

'Is everything loaded on the horses?' Jack asked.

'All loaded and ready to go,' Grant replied.

'I'll be back shortly, then,' said Jack.

He ran back to the windmill and dropped a lighted match on the pile of hay at the foot of each of its four timber legs. Then he ran back to the others, mounted his horse, and they rode off towards the homesteads. When they had covered half a mile they paused to look back. The glow of the fire was clearly visible through the darkness.

When they reached the Lee homestead they dug a large hole and buried all the items they had taken from the ranch buildings. Then they assembled in the house.

'I don't reckon they'll bother us for a while,' said Jack. 'There's no doubt we've left them in a bit of a fix specially with them not being able to fasten their saddles properly on their horses. It's going to take them quite a while to get back to normal.

'All the same, I reckon we'd better carry on with lookouts, like we've been doing up to now.'

'What d'you think Duff'll do now?' asked Grant. 'I reckon he's mighty riled about what's happened and he'll be sure that we're the ones who did the damage.'

'You're right,' Jack replied, 'but even though he's pretty mad he knows that he'll have to put things right at the ranch before he makes another move against us. It could be that he decides to leave us alone now. My guess is that he won't. All we can do is wait and see what happens, and keep an eye out for trouble all the time.'

The following day the men, apart from the lookout, worked on the homesteads. There were no sightings of Box D hands. After dark, Jack rode into Monroe, and leaving his horse just outside town he walked un-observed to the doctor's house and knocked on the door. Shannon let him in.

'How's Lee?' asked Jack.

'Coming along fine,' the doctor replied. 'I reckon he's well out of danger now.'

He took Jack into the room where Lee was lying and listened while Jack told the settler about the previous night's operation.

'That explains a lot,' said Shannon, when Jack had finished.

He told Jack that during the morning of that day, a buckboard with a makeshift harness had come into town from the Box D. The storekeeper and liveryman had told him that the two hands on board had come into Monroe with the intention of buying kitchen utensils, cinches, head stalls and bits, and also rope, but it turned out that the quantities they required were far above what the store and livery stable could supply at short notice.

'That's good,' said Jack. 'It looks like it's going to be a while before Duff gets things back into shape.'

Before leaving, he told Lee that he was about to ride out to the ravine to let his wife know that he was well on the way to recovery, and to tell all the women about the present situation in the valley.

It was half an hour before midnight when he arrived at the ravine. He called out to

Miriam Farrell, who was taking her turn at standing guard, and while she was waking the women he went to the shack and woke Benson.

When the women came to the shack, Jack told Ruth Lee about her husband's satisfactory progress at the doctor's house. Then he told the women about the events of the previous night and the subsequent visit of the two Box D hands to Monroe.

'You sure had a busy time at the ranch,' said Benson. 'I guess Duff's sorry he ever threatened you. Maybe he'll leave the homesteads alone now.'

'That's what I'm hoping,' said Jack. 'We'll just have to wait and see. Until we know one way or the other, you ladies had better stay here.'

'The longer they stay here, the better for me,' smiled Benson. 'I ain't fed so well for a long time. And I'm getting to like the company.'

On the Box D Ranch, the mayhem during

the nocturnal visit of Jack and the settlers had been entirely unexpected by Duff. Although almost beside himself with rage when the damage and thefts were discovered, he knew that his first priority was to put in hand arrangements to get the ranch functioning properly again, thereby ensuring the welfare of his cattle.

A shopping expedition to Monroe enabled three saddle horses to be equipped for riding and had produced a small quantity of rope and a few small kitchen utensils, all a long way short of the total requirements.

At the ranch the stove was so badly damaged that it was beyond repair, and cooking had to be done over an open air fire. The windmill tower had collapsed and timber was required to rebuild it. Meanwhile, the hands had to carry up water from the river. Replacements of the burnt and damaged winter hay was a necessity.

Duff dispatched a rider to Amarillo, some ninety miles distant to the south, to purchase all that was necessary to restore the quantities of missing items to their former levels, and to rebuild the windmill and replace the stove. All the foregoing items were to be hauled post-haste to the ranch by freight wagon.

Duff expected that the freight would arrive at the ranch in around fourteen days. He decided that while waiting for it to turn up, he would strike a blow at the homesteaders who had dared to attack him so effectively on his own ground.

He sent for one of his hands, a half-breed called Parker. He had taken on Parker four years previously because of his uncanny ability in the art of stalking and tracking, talents which had been of great use to the rancher when engaged on certain cattle-stealing operations.

It was Parker who had earlier shot and wounded Lee from the north side of the river. He had also been responsible, on an earlier occasion, for the death of Clem Farrell. Parker, under orders from Duff, had stopped the settler when he was riding into town, had pistol-whipped him and dropped his body into the gorge where it was found.

Duff told Parker to go to the Lee homestead on foot after dark, not along the main trail, but well south of it, so that he could approach the homestead from the south when he came abreast of it. He was to arrive soon after midnight.

'Nelson and the settlers are probably at Lee's place,' said Duff. 'Watch out for guards and if you get a chance to kill any of them without getting caught, do it. I expect you to get one at least.'

Parker arrived at a point fifty yards south of Lee's homestead at twenty five minutes past midnight. Soundlessly, he crawled along the ground towards the homestead, pausing now and again to listen. So far, there was no sign of a guard.

He crossed the trail which ran past the homesteads, halted for a while, then crawled on towards the house, whose outline he could see directly ahead of him. No lights were showing. Reaching the wall of the house he circled it cautiously without seeing a guard. Deciding that none had been posted, he went to the door, slowly opened it, and slipped through the doorway.

Inside the house, Grant and Dixon were asleep in the two bedrooms and Jack was lying on the floor of the living-room. Fisher was in the barn loft.

Jack lying on his side facing the outside door, was awakened by a faint creak and a slight draught as the door slowly opened. He opened his eyes, but did not move his body. In the faint light coming from the slowly-burning stove he saw a man step silently into the room and carefully close the door behind him. He knew it was not Fisher, who would have called out before entering.

The half-breed stood just inside the door and looked around the room. He saw the motionless blanket-covered figure lying on the floor and glided towards it, raising his right arm.

He bent over Jack and brought his arm

down just as Jack quickly twisted his body sideways and reached for the Peacemaker lying by his side on the floor. The knife in Parker's hand, intended to penetrate deep into Jack's chest, gashed the side of his upper arm. The half-breed raised his arm again, but before he could bring the knife down once more Jack raised and cocked the Peacemaker and shot him through the head.

The sound of the shot brought Grant and Dixon into the room as Jack was lighting a lamp. They looked down at the body on the floor.

'That's Parker,' said Dixon, 'one of the Box D hands.'

'So,' said Jack, 'it looks like the fight's not over yet. This man did his best to kill me. I'll go and tell Fisher what's happened. I expect he heard the shot. And I'll check whether there are any more Box D hands around, though I doubt it. If there had been, they'd have all come into the house together.'

Jack found no sign of further intruders outside, and going into the barn he told

Fisher about the shooting of Parker. Then he returned to the house and took a look at his left arm. The gash from the knife was not very deep and Grant bathed the wound and bandaged it for him.

'What do we do with Parker?' asked Dixon.

'We'll carry him off the homestead,' said Jack, 'and bury him on the other side of the trail. It'll give Duff something to think about when Parker doesn't turn up at the ranch.

'It looks like Duff's still hell bent on taking the homesteads over. Maybe he needs another reminder that he can't always have just what he wants. Come daylight, I'm going to ride into Monroe for a talk with Ranger, the storekeeper.'

When Jack reached town there was no sign of the presence of any Box D ranch hands. He rode up to the store and went inside. Ranger, stacking some goods behind the counter, was alone. Jack gave him the details of the raid on the Box D, which the storekeeper had already heard of from the doctor, but he didn't mention Parker's subsequent visit to the Lee homestead.

Ranger told Jack that on the previous day he and the liveryman had been able to supply only a very small proportion of the items that Duff wanted. They had told Duff's man to tell the rancher that the nearest place they could be sure of getting everything they wanted was Amarillo.

'Two hours after the men left,' said Ranger, 'I saw one of the hands called Green riding fast through town. He was heading south after he cleared the buildings, and I'm willing to bet that he was heading for Amarillo to buy the things that Duff wants and have them freighted back here as quickly as possible.'

'You say it was yesterday when you saw Green riding south?' asked Jack.

'That's right,' replied Ranger.

'When would you expect the freight to be delivered to the Box D?' asked Jack.

The storekeeper scratched his head.

'Allowing for the time it takes Green to ride to Amarillo, collect the supplies, and organize a freight wagon,' he said, 'and assuming the wagon is hauled by a mule team, my guess is that it'll arrive at the Box D not earlier than thirteen days from today.'

'Thanks,' said Jack, then requested a certain item from the storekeeper. Ranger went out to a small shed standing behind the store, and came back shortly after with a small canvas bag which he handed to Jack.

Jack left the store and went along to the doctor's house to see how Lee was progressing. He found that the homesteader's condition was rapidly improving. He asked Shannon to take a look at the knife cut on his own arm, which was paining him a little.

Shannon took the bandage off and examined the gash.

'Could do with a few stitches,' he said. 'I'll put them in now and bandage it up again. It should heal up fine.'

After a few more words with Lee and the doctor, Jack rode off along the trail which led south through the Panhandle, and which eventually reached Amarillo. He had ridden just over nine miles when he stopped for several minutes close to a large rock outcrop standing at the top of a steep rise. He looked ahead, then backwards along the trail, then to each side. Then, after circling the outcrop, he rode back to the homestead.

SIX

Over the following days Jack and the settlers continued with their work on the home-steads, keeping the lookout positions manned day and night. Jack, on a visit to town, heard from Doc Shannon that a Box D hand had been asking around town whether anyone had seen Parker recently.

Since the encounter with Parker, Jack and the settlers had discussed their next move against Duff, and eleven days after the death of the half-breed, Jack and Grant left the homesteads in the morning. Bypassing Monroe, they joined the trail leading in the direction of Amarillo and rode south along it.

When they arrived at the outcrop that Jack had reached when he rode out just after Parker's death, they stopped and dismounted.

'This is the place,' said Jack. 'I figure it's just right for an ambush. There's a recess at the back of the outcrop where we can hide with the horses while we watch out for the freight wagon. With the glasses, we should be able to spot it well before it gets anywhere near here.'

They settled down to their vigil after discussing a plan which would enable them to capture the wagon. But it was not until late afternoon on the following day that Grant, looking south along the trail through the glasses, saw a wagon heading towards them. He called out to Jack and handed the glasses over.

Watching the wagon, Jack could see, as it drew closer, that it was being pulled by three pairs of mules, with the muleskinner riding on one of the last pair. Two men on horseback were accompanying the wagon.

'I reckon that's the wagon we're waiting for,' said Jack, 'but it ain't going to be quite as easy as we thought. We're up against the muleskinner and two other men. One of them's Green, I guess, and maybe the other man's there to help him guard the wagon. But we'll stick to the plan we worked out. You take care of the muleskinner like we agreed and I'll see to the others.'

Green's companion was, in fact, a man he had hired both to help him escort the wagon, and also, as an expert in such matters, to supervise the rebuilding of the windmill at the Box D.

Hiding in the large recess at the rear of the outcrop, Jack and Grant watched the approaching wagon, which slowed down as it started to climb the slope leading to their position. The two riders were side by side, abreast of the middle of the wagon, and well behind the muleskinner.

When the wagon, moving quite slowly now, had just passed the outcrop, Jack and Grant slipped out of their hiding place and ran on to the trail behind it.

Holding his Peacemaker, Jack ran up behind the two riders, the sound of his footsteps drowned by the noise of the moving wagon. When he had reached a point close behind them, he fired a shot in the air and called on them to stop and put up their hands.

Startled, the two riders stopped and turned in the saddle. They saw Jack behind them, holding a revolver which was pointing in their direction. Green made a move towards his gun, but cancelled it when a bullet from Jack's Peacemaker hit the high crown of his Texas hat and jerked it from his head. The two men raised their hands.

Meanwhile, Grant had run up behind the wagon and along the far side of it, then on until he was abreast of the muleskinner, and to the man's right. The teamster was looking back over his left shoulder towards the sound of the revolver shot, when Grant called out to him to stop the team.

The muleskinner looked into the two barrels of Grant's shotgun and obeyed the order with alacrity. When the wagon rolled to a halt Grant kept the teamster covered and told him to stay where he was.

By this time Jack had disarmed the two riders and had ordered them to dismount and walk forward until they were abreast of the muleskinner, who was unarmed. He ordered the teamster to dismount, then waited until Grant joined him, when they took the three prisoners to the recess in the outcrop.

Once there, they tied the hands of the three men with rope they had brought with them, and Jack ordered them to sit down. Green spoke.

'You ain't going to get away with this, Nelson,' he said. 'If this wagon don't get through, you and all those settlers are going to be in deep trouble. Mr Duff's going to take it real bad, and there's no knowing what he'll do.'

'Anything, I expect,' replied Jack, 'including murder. But this is one time a big rancher ain't going to be allowed to ride roughshod over legitimate settlers who just want to be left alone.'

Leaving Grant to guard the prisoners, Jack

went to look at the contents of the freight wagon. He found that it contained the timber and parts necessary for bringing the windmill into working order again; cinches, bridles and rope; kitchen utensils and a complete new stove.

He took the saddles and bridles off the horses of Green and his companion and threw them into the wagon. Then he unhitched the mules and led three of them to the back of the outcrop.

He ordered the three prisoners to mount the mules. Then he and Grant mounted their horses, and Grant led the three mules along the trail north, with Jack bringing up the rear and leading the three remaining mules and the two unsaddled horses.

Fifty yards along the trail Jack called on Grant to stop and wait. He twisted round and freed the small canvas bag which was tied behind his saddle, and which he had earlier obtained from Ranger, the store-keeper in Monroe. Holding his shotgun, Grant turned his horse to face the three prisoners, while Jack rode quickly back to the wagon.

He dismounted and climbed up inside it. From the bag he was carrying he took out three sticks of dynamite, with fuse cords cut to a carefully calculated length. Striking a match, he lit the three fuse cords, then dropped one stick inside the stove, and the other two in the middle of the wagon.

Returning to his horse, he mounted and rode back to Grant, then turned as the sound of three explosions, in quick succession, reached him.

Green and the muleskinner cursed at the spectacle as the wagon lost its top and the sides buckled outwards. Almost immediately, what was left of the wagon, together with its contents, was engulfed in flames. The fire was still burning fiercely as they headed north again, leaving the spare mules and horses behind.

It was after midnight when they found themselves approaching Monroe. They circled the town at a distance and rode into the valley, where they paused for a few minutes while Jack gagged the three prisoners. Then they headed for the Box D ranch buildings.

Jack was certain that Duff would have posted night guards, and he headed for the side of the corral remote from the ranch buildings. He was sure that in the darkness they would not be spotted there.

They all dismounted, and Jack and Grant tied the three prisoners firmly to the rails of the corral fence. They tethered the three mules to the rails, then headed for the homestead. They found Fisher on guard at a prearranged point near the Lee homestead, and called out to him as they approached.

They told him briefly about the success of their mission, then rode on to the house, where they woke Randle and Dixon and told them the same story, before getting some sleep themselves.

In the morning they all assembled for breakfast and Jack and Grant gave the others the full story of the destruction of the freight wagon and its contents. Then Jack asked whether any Box D men had been seen around the homesteads during their absence.

'Nary a one,' said Dixon. 'What d'you think Duff's next move will be?'

'He's got to arrange for another shipment of the items that were in that wagon,' replied Jack. 'Without those things he just can't operate like he needs to. But next time, I reckon the wagon'll be so well guarded that there'll be no chance at all of us capturing it again.

'It does mean that we've probably got about a couple of weeks before Duff tries to make any more trouble for us. We'll just have to stay on our guard and see what happens. Meantime, one of us had better ride out to the women tonight, to tell them how things stand.'

'*I'll* do that,' said Randle, 'and I'll take some more provisions for them.'

On the Box D, Miller, the night guard stationed outside the house, watched the sun lift over some high ground to the east, and looked forward to the breakfast he expected to be eating in half an hour's time.

As he looked around, his attention was caught by something unusual on the far side of the corral. There appeared to be some animals standing there and some objects up against the rails.

He called out to the other night guard, Jackson, who was stationed outside the bunkhouse, and gestured towards the corral. Then both the men ran over and discovered the three mules and the three men tied to the rails.

Duff was almost speechless with rage when he learnt of the loss of the shipment he had so eagerly been awaiting. When he had calmed down a little, he ordered Green to ride again to Amarillo and arrange for an identical shipment to the one which had just been destroyed. He told Green to hire an adequate guard for the shipment on its journey to the ranch.

When Green had departed, after taking a

quick meal, the rancher went into the house, sat at his desk, and wrote on a sheet of paper for a time. He folded the sheet, put it in an envelope, and called in his son Brad, who was now almost fully recovered from the shoulder injury inflicted on him by Jack.

'What're we going to do about them settlers?' asked Brad. 'I never figured they'd be able to cause us this much trouble.'

'The reason for that,' said his father, 'is because Nelson's clearly running the show. And right now, there ain't much we can do to get back at them. I figured that Parker would get rid of Nelson for us, but it's clear now that he failed. And I have a feeling that we ain't going to see Parker again.'

He handed the envelope to his son, giving him instructions as to the person to whom it must be delivered at the earliest possible moment. Shortly after, Brad Duff rode away from the ranch at a fast pace in an easterly direction.

On the fifth day after his departure, the rancher's son arrived back at the Box D

ranch house accompanied by a tough-look-
ing quartet led by an outlaw called Quincy
Daley. Daley and the three members of his
gang were wanted by the law for numerous
robberies and murders in Kansas, Nebraska
and Indian Territory.

Willard Duff had been associated with the
gang for a time, before starting on his career
as a rancher, with rustling activities as a
sideline.

Daley was a big man, bearded, with a bleak
face showing a knife scar on one cheek.
Looking at him, it was easy to believe the
stories one heard of his readiness to murder
anyone who interfered with his illegal activities. His three companions, Parkin, Fell and
Lorimer, were all unscrupulous characters,
cast in the same mould as their leader.

Willard Duff was waiting outside the door
of the house when they rode up and
dismounted. The rancher greeted Daley and
took him into the house while his son took
the others to the bunkhouse.

'I'm sure glad,' said the rancher, 'that Brad

found you at the hideout in Indian Territory. I reckon he's told you about the problem we have here?'

'He has,' said Daley, 'and I've got to say I was plumb surprised to hear that a bunch of nesters had managed to put you in such a fix.'

'It's all because of a stranger called Jack Nelson,' said Duffy. 'He tied in with the homesteaders and I'm pretty sure he's telling them what to do.'

'Jack Nelson, you say,' said Daley, thoughtfully... 'I met up with a Jack Nelson a while back when we were operating in Kansas. He was sheriff of Ford County. Twice, he very nearly caught up with us after a robbery and I figured we'd better move out of his territory. What does this Jack Nelson look like?'

After the rancher had given Daley a detailed description of Jack, the outlaw told the rancher and his son, who had just come into the room, that the Jack Nelson who was helping the homesteaders was, without doubt, the sheriff he had known in Ford County.

'I didn't know he'd quit Kansas,' said Daley, 'and I'm wondering how he comes to be in these parts.'

'Nobody seems to know,' said the rancher, 'but the fact is, he's here, and I want him and the settlers out of the valley. That's why I sent for you. You can count on my men for help if you need it.'

'We'll see,' said Daley. 'Are all the settlers still working their homesteads?'

'All except one called Lee,' replied Duff, who was paying an old-timer in town called Harker for any information he could give the rancher about the movements of Jack and the settlers. 'Lee was shot by one of my men and he's laid up at the doctor's house. Seems like he'll soon be all right.

'As for the others, I reckon they're all staying together in one of the homesteads during the night, with guards posted. And one interesting thing I've heard is the women and children ain't been seen, either in town or around the homesteads, for more'n a week. Which makes me wonder where they are.'

'That *is* interesting,' said Daley. 'I reckon one of the first things for me and my men to do is to find out just where they are. I've always noticed that the stubbornnest men are likely to cave in if their families are threatened. I can't understand it myself, but it's a sort of weak spot they seem to have. I take it that nobody apart from the men on this ranch knows that we're here?'

'That's right,' replied the rancher.

'Good,' said Daley. 'Let's keep it that way as long as we can. It's near certain,' he went on, 'that the women and children have been taken out of the valley, but not so far out that the settlers can't easily keep in touch with them. So what me and my men are going to do tomorrow is split up, and each of us will comb a quarter of the area outside the valley and close to it. When we've done that we'll come back here. If one of us *does* spot them, he'll be sure not to let them know it. If they are spotted, we'll decide then what to do next.'

SEVEN

The following morning, out of sight of Monroe and the homesteads, Daley and his men rode out of the valley and commenced their search of the area allocated to them. Their search was painstaking and they took full advantage of any cover available.

By late afternoon Daley, Parkin and Lorimer had all completed a fruitless search of their area and were heading back to the ranch. Fell, who was covering the western section of the area north of the valley, had almost completed his search and was standing with his horse inside a small grove of trees, looking to the west.

He started to lead his horse out of the grove, with the intention of heading back to the Box D, then suddenly halted as a slight movement to the north caught his attention.

A figure, which looked like that of a woman, had moved out from behind a large rock and stood looking round for a short while. Then she retreated out of sight.

Fell could see that if he approached any closer to the woman from any direction he would be spotted, and he decided to wait where he was until after dark. An hour after sundown he rode out of the grove and headed towards the place where he had seen the woman.

With still some distance to go he dismounted and tethered his horse. On foot, he stealthily circled, at a distance, the position at which he had seen the woman standing. Suddenly, he found himself close to the top of the wall of a small ravine. He lay down and looked over the edge.

He could hear the faint sounds of children's voices down below and could see two small fires burning, with women moving around them. Then, for a brief instant, he saw what looked like the figure of a man. He felt reasonably confident that he had discovered the whereabouts of the settlers' women and children.

He climbed down into the ravine and moved closer to the fires. He could now see the women and children clearly. Cautiously, he explored the ravine, taking advantage of the darkness away from the fires. He saw the shack, the tents and the three buckboards, also the mule and burro. But there was no sign that any horses were present.

Fell climbed out of the ravine, returned to his horse, and rode back to the Box D. He joined Daley and the Duffs in the ranch house and told them of his discovery.

'How many women and children did you see?' asked Willard Duff.

'As far as I could tell,' replied Fell, 'there were six women and six children, and I thought I caught a glimpse of a man, but I ain't sure. Could have been a prospector, on account of the mule and the burro.'

'Those numbers sound about right for the women and children,' said the rancher. 'What do we do now?'

'The four of us,' said Daley, 'will ride out there right now, and before dawn we'll deal with the guard and take the place over. We should be able to hold out there against anything the nesters can throw at us. Not that I think they'd attack us. They'd be too worried about the women and children for that.

'When we've taken the ravine over you can get a message to the homesteaders that the women and children are being held in the ravine, and that as soon as your supplies arrive from Amarillo the men have got to be ready to be escorted out of the valley by your hands to some place well away from here, where their families will be waiting for them. We can decide where that place is later.

'And you can say that the ravine is well guarded and the women and children are liable to suffer if anybody tries to free them.'

'You want any help to guard those people in there?' asked the rancher.

Daley raised his eyebrows in surprise at

the question.

'Six women, six children, and maybe one prospector,' he said ironically. 'I figure the four of us might just be able to handle the situation.'

Daley and his men left shortly after, keeping well clear of the homesteads. It was an hour and a half before dawn by the time they reached the point where Fell had tethered his horse the previous evening.

There, the others waited, while Fell, taking advantage of any cover available, slowly advanced on the position at which he had seen a guard the previous evening. Finally, moving silently on all fours, he came close to the rock from behind which he had seen the woman emerge on his first visit. He stopped and lay flat on the ground, listening intently.

Several minutes later he heard a cough, then the sound of somebody moving. Miriam Farrell, carrying a rifle, stepped out from behind the rock and stood silhouetted against the night sky, looking in his direction. He lay motionless, and a few minutes later she turned and looked in the opposite direction.

Silently, Fell rose and crept up behind Miriam. At the last moment she sensed his presence, but it was too late. He struck her on the back of the head with the barrel of his six-shooter, and while she was temporarily stunned he gagged her.

Then he struck a match and waved it sideways a few times, a signal to Daley and the others that it was safe for them to join him. When they did so, they tied Miriam, who was now conscious, hand and foot, and laid her on the ground. Then, leaving her there, the four outlaws made their way into the ravine.

They headed first for the shack, where the old prospector, Hiram Benson, was sleeping. Daley opened the door and went inside, leaving his men to watch the tents. Inside the shack Daley heard the sound of heavy breathing. He struck a match and lit a lamp standing on a table. Benson, lying on a bunk on the far side of the shack, stirred, and his eyes opened as he rolled over to look towards the light.

Seeing Daley, he reached for the shotgun hanging on the wall close to the bunk and started bringing it round to bear on the outlaw. But before he could complete the move, Daley shot him through the head.

The sound of the shot woke the women and children, and as they came out of the tents they were covered by Daley's men and were ordered to go into the shack. The tents were then searched for weapons.

Inside the shack the women stood in silence, badly shaken by the sight of the dead body of Benson, whom they had come to look on as a friend. Three of the children started crying and were comforted by their mothers. Miriam, shaken by her ordeal, but not badly injured, was brought down from the lookout point to the shack to join the other women. Then Daley addressed them.

'My name's Daley,' he said. 'Me and my men are aiming to stay here for a spell to hold you women and children in the ravine. Mr Duff figures to persuade your menfolk that it'll be best for everybody if they leave their homesteads and move out of the valley for good. As soon as they've done that you'll be taken to join up with them again.

'And don't count on anybody trying to rescue you. Your menfolk know what'll happen to you here if they try anything like that. And another thing, any of you caught trying to escape'll be shot like this man here.'

He pointed to Benson, lying on his blood-soaked bunk.

Miriam Farrell, her head still throbbing from the effects of the blow she had received, spoke up.

'You're murderers!' she said. 'This man ain't done you no wrong. You didn't have to kill him.'

'Is that so?' said Daley. 'He had the notion to ventilate me with that shotgun. That's enough for me.'

He ordered the women to go back to their

tents with the children and to carry on with their normal routine. He said he expected them to prepare meals for him and his three companions.

When the women had left, Daley spoke to his men.

'These women ain't to be touched,' he said. 'I know it's going to be hard for you, 'specially for Lorimer here, but that's how it has to be.'

Lorimer, a tall, swarthy man, with a broken front tooth, looked disappointed. His liking for female company was well known to his companions.

'And about the guarding arrangements,' Daley went on, 'we're not going to take any chances. Day and night, we'll have one man, relieved every four hours, at the top of the ravine wall, near the entrance. Then, at night, we'll have an extra guard, relieved every four hours, watching the tents and keeping a fire going.'

Miriam's tent was nearby and she clearly heard Daley's orders to his men.

A little later, as dawn was breaking, and the women stood discussing the situation, Daley's men carried Benson's body a little way up the ravine and started digging a hole in which to bury him.

'It looks like we're beat, don't it?' said Ethel Grant. 'The men ain't got no choice but to leave.'

'That's the way it looks,' agreed Miriam, 'but don't forget we've got Jack Nelson on our side. He and the menfolk have given Duff plenty of trouble up to now. I can't see just what, at the moment, but maybe there's something we can do here to help them.

'For the time being we'd better just carry on as we were before. There's no point in anybody trying to escape without a proper plan. These men are murderers.'

Daley came out of the shack and looked at the group of women. He walked up to May Dixon who was wearing a brightly-coloured shawl, of a distinctive pattern, against the morning chill. He took it from her and walked over to Parkin, one of his men.

'Leave the others to finish the burying,' he said, 'and ride to the Box D. Tell Duff that the women and children have been taken prisoner and an old prospector in the ravine with them has been killed and buried. Tell Duff that there's no need for him or his men to contact us in the ravine until the men on the homesteads have agreed to move out of the valley. When you've done that, ride back here.'

Duff received the news with some elation and he decided to ride out to the homesteads immediately, with his son. They were spotted by the lookout Grant when they were still some distance away, and when they approached the Lee homestead, with hands raised, Jack and the settlers, all armed, were standing on the trail awaiting them.

The two Duffs stopped just within speaking distance of Jack and the others. The rancher spoke.

'I've come to let you men know,' he said, 'that your wives and children have been found in that ravine outside the valley north-west of here, and they're now being guarded by four friends of mine, the Daley gang. They're all professional gunfighters. I'm sure you've heard of them, Nelson. But just in case you think I'm bluffing, take a look at this.'

From a bag attached to his saddle-horn he pulled out a folded shawl and opened it for the men in front of him to see.

'That's May's!' shouted Dixon. 'Damn you, Duff! I've a mind to shoot you down right now.'

'That wouldn't be wise,' said the rancher. 'Anything happens to me, and somebody in that ravine is going to suffer. And the same applies if you're foolish enough to try and rescue the women and children. The slightest sign of any of you coming near to the ravine or to the Box D buildings, day or night, and your families will pay the penalty.'

'What is it you want, Duff?' asked Jack.

'As you probably know,' said Duff, 'I'm

expecting a shipment of goods from Amarillo before long. After it's arrived, my men will escort all you men out of the valley. At the same time my friends in the ravine will take your wives and children to meet up with you some place a long way from here. And if any of you try to get back into the valley, you'll be shot.'

'You must know,' said Jack, 'that what you're doing is against the law.'

'*I'm* the law around here,' said Duff, 'and after the damage you've done to my property, I reckon I'm letting you off lightly.'

Privately, he had already decided that even though the other men went free, Jack would be eliminated.

Dismayed and apprehensive, Jack and his companions watched as Duff and his son turned and rode off towards the ranch.

'I know the Daley gang,' said Jack. 'All of them are dangerous killers and outlaws. I nearly caught up with them a couple of times when I was a lawman in Kansas. If they're guarding the women and children in that ravine, I'd say that the chances of us rescuing them are practically nil.'

'What can we do, then?' asked Dixon.

'Nothing just now that I can think of,' Jack replied. 'Not without risking harm coming to the women and children. All we can do is wait here until Duff gets his men fully operational again. I know it's hard to take, but I can't see any other way.'

EIGHT

As Jack was speaking, the women in the ravine were sitting on the ground outside Miriam Farrell's tent, discussing the situation.

'I've been thinking,' said Miriam, 'that maybe there's a way we can get the better of these four villains. But we'll all have to work together.'

She told them what she had overheard about Daley's plans for the posting of guards. Then she turned to May Dixon, a slim, blonde, good-looking woman in her late twenties.

'May,' she said. 'Have you noticed the way that man Lorimer looks at you?'

'I have,' said May, 'and I don't like it one little bit.'

'I don't blame you,' said Miriam, 'but it's

116

clear he's attracted to you, and from what I heard Daley say, he's a man who craves female company. Maybe, if you're willing to play along, we can use that fact to help us get free.'

'What you're asking me to do, Miriam,' said May, 'makes me feel sick inside, but for the sake of all of us, I'm willing to give it a try. What's your plan?'

Miriam went into the details of her scheme, while the other women listened intently. Then, for the next half hour, they discussed it, made a few minor changes, and decided to go ahead. The role to be played by each of the women was then settled.

Miriam was not surprised at their decision. These women were all fighters by nature, their characters moulded and tempered by the hardships of life on the frontier.

During the afternoon Lorimer spent most of his time sitting between the shack and the tents watching the women, particularly May Dixon. Several times she passed close by him, looked at him shyly and smiled, but did not speak.

A little suspicious at first, Lorimer's self-esteem soon convinced him that this was the latest in a long line of females who had succumbed to his charms. He grinned back at May the next time she passed by.

After dark, while Fell stood guard over the entrance to the ravine, the other three outlaws sat by one of the fires. Then, at ten o'clock, Fell walked up to the fire and Parkin walked off to replace him, shouting back that he would return at two o'clock in the morning to wake the next man on guard.

To the relief of Miriam and May, who were peeping out of their tents, Daley and Fell went inside the shack, leaving Lorimer on guard over the tents. They figured that Lorimer and Parkin would be at their posts until two o'clock in the morning, when they were due to be relieved.

At a quarter past one in the morning, Miriam saw May open the flap of her tent and step outside. A moon, covered with thin cloud, was giving some light. She was wearing a dressing-gown over her nightdress and was carrying a basket. Half-dozing, Lorimer started as he saw her, and got to his feet as she approached him.

She stopped in front of him, smiling, then moved round him so that she was facing Miriam's tent. He turned to face her, thinking that she ranked pretty high on the list of good-looking women he had encountered over the years.

Stealthily, unobserved by Lorimer, Miriam left her tent, moved round to the back of it, and ran silently into the darkness, heading up the ravine. She was carrying some objects in her hand. Fortunately for the women's plan, Parkin, from his lookout point, was unable to see, even in daylight, the shack and the tents down in the ravine.

'I've just remembered,' said May to Lorimer, 'I laid some washing out this afternoon in the sun, a little way up the ravine. It's on that big boulder over there, at the side of the ravine. I aim to go and collect it. I was wondering if you'd come along with me. It's a bit scary out there in the dark.'

Lorimer grinned. 'I ain't got no choice,' he said. 'I've got to be sure you come back here. Let's go.'

They walked slowly out of the light of the fire and up the ravine. Lorimer, carrying his rifle, followed close behind May. She headed straight for a large, roundish boulder, about five feet high and eight feet in diameter, standing close to the wall of the ravine.

Lorimer could see some garments draped on top of the boulder. May lifted them off and dropped them into the basket which she had handed to the outlaw. When she had finished, Lorimer laid the basket on the ground, dropped his rifle, and grabbed May, pressing her against the boulder, and trying forcibly to remove her dressing-gown.

Unseen by the outlaw, Miriam slipped out from behind the boulder and approached Lorimer from the rear. She was carrying a heavy mallet which had been supplied with the tents for driving the fixing pegs into the ground.

While passing through a Kansas cattle town two years earlier, on their way to the Panhandle, Miriam and her husband had witnessed the taming – by a respected town marshal – of a drunken, unruly cowboy waving a pistol. Rather than shoot the man down, the marshal had pistol-whipped him over the head, and dragged him off sense-less, to the jail.

Miriam figured that she could achieve the same result with the mallet. She raised it and struck Lorimer forcibly just above the right ear. The outlaw dropped like a log and the two women hurriedly gagged him and thoroughly trussed him with some rope which had been left in one of the buck-boards.

Then, taking the outlaw's six-gun and rifle with them, they left Lorimer where he was lying and crossed to the place where four horses were tethered. They picked up the four lariats lying near the saddles. Then they returned to the tents. The time was twenty-five minutes before two o'clock.

They told the other women that all was going according to plan so far, and Ethel Grant left her tent to join them. All three headed for the entrance to the ravine, keeping well out of sight of the lookout position.

They knew the route that the lookout took when returning to the shack. He would climb down until he was able to enter the mouth of the ravine, keeping close to the steep wall on the north side. In this wall was a recess into which the three women slipped and hid in the shadows.

While awaiting the appearance of Parkin, they talked only in whispers, all the time aware that if Daley or Fell happened to wake up and discover the absence of Lorimer from his post, their plan would surely fail.

It was a few minutes before two o'clock when they heard the sound of Parkin's footsteps approaching their position. They let him pass by the recess, then all three women ran out and launched themselves at him from the rear.

Hearing a slight sound behind him, Parkin, a short, slim man, started to turn. But he was too late. He crashed down onto his face and was pinned to the ground by the three women before he could even think of retaliation. Miriam forcibly jammed the muzzle of Lorimer's six-gun into the side of the outlaw's neck.

'Give us any trouble, and you're dead,' she said, forcing the muzzle even further into the flesh, while the other women took his weapons.

Parkin gave up any attempt to struggle, and lay motionless.

May forced a gag into his mouth and tied it tightly at the back of his neck. Then, while Miriam kept the gun at his neck, the other two women trussed him thoroughly with the rope they had brought with them.

They left Parkin in the recess and returned to the other women, carrying Parkin's rifle and six-gun with them. Leaving Ellen Fisher behind to keep an eye on the children, the other five women walked up to the shack.

Miriam was carrying a six-gun and a lighted oil lamp with the wick turned well down. May was carrying a six-gun, and two of the other women were carrying rifles.

Quietly, Miriam opened the door of the shack and entered, followed by her four companions. She placed the lamp on a table and they stood looking at the two men lying sound asleep on the two bunks against the rear wall of the shack.

Miriam picked up the two gunbelts from the floor near the bunks, while May lifted Hiram Benson's shotgun off the wall.

The weapons, except for one revolver which was taken by one of the women, were quietly laid on the ground outside the shack.

Miriam fired a shot from her revolver into the wall of the shack close to the heads of the two sleeping men. Galvanized into action, they reached for their guns, found them missing, and sat bolt upright on their bunks. Their eyes goggled as they saw the five women, all holding weapons pointing in their direction.

Miriam turned up the wick of the lamp.

'What we're going to do, Daley,' she said, 'is tie you two up well and good, just like we've already tied up your two men outside. You can be the first. Lie down!'

Daley, finding it hard to believe that he was in such a situation, was slow in complying. Miriam fired, and the bullet from her six-gun fanned Daley's cheek and buried itself in the wall behind his head.

The bullet had passed a lot closer to the outlaw's head than Miriam had intended, but Daley didn't know that. He sank down on the bunk and Miriam held the barrel of her revolver against his temple while two of the women soundly trussed him. The other two women had their weapons pointed at Fell.

When Daley had been attended to, the same procedure was adopted for Fell. The two men were left on their bunks while the women went outside to discuss the next move.

'One thing's certain,' said Miriam. 'These men are dangerous and they'll have to be closely watched all the time. The ropes will have to come off now and then, but we'll only do it on one of them at a time, and we'll keep that one well covered. I don't reckon we need to feed them. It won't hurt them to do without food for a day or two. We'll just pour a drop of water into their mouths every now and again.'

'Tell us again, Miriam,' said Ruth Lee, 'about that place we're taking them to.'

'Like I told you before,' said Miriam, 'it's a town over in Indian Territory, maybe a little under fifty miles from here. It's called Tipawa. We passed through it about two years ago when we were driving our wagon out here. The day before we got there the Daley gang had robbed the bank and killed the cashier and a woman who happened to be on the street when they were making their getaway.

'I figured that if we took Daley and his men there, the folks in town would jump at the chance to hold them while they got word to the US Marshal in Fort Smith to send deputies to pick them up. We should get there in two or three days.'

'When do we leave?' asked Ethel Grant, 'and how do we let the men know we're free?'

'We'll leave at daylight,' said Miriam, 'and we'll send word to the men as soon as we reach Tipawa. I reckon it'll be safer that way.'

Working together, the women dragged Daley and Fell out of the shack, then went for Parkin and Lorimer in turn, and dragged them up to lay beside their leader. The outlaws lay fuming as they watched the women preparing for their departure.

When dawn came the outlaws were unceremoniously heaved up by the women and cramped on to the floor of one of the buckboards. The tents and provisions were thrown in with them. The children climbed on to the other buckboard.

The four outlaws' horses were hitched to the buckboards, one pair to each, and Benson's mule and burrow were tied behind one of the buckboards. A rough cross was fashioned and hammered into the ground at the head of the prospector's grave. His name and date of death were marked on the cross.

With the women sitting on the seats of the buckboards, they set off, heading east, with the buckboard carrying the outlaws in the lead.

Making the best time they could, they spent two nights on the trail and for the whole journey the women kept the outlaws under constant surveillance, not allowing them the slightest chance of escape, and gagging them whenever their language became too profane or threatening.

It was eleven o'clock on the morning of a clear, sunny day when the buckboards rolled into Tipawa.

NINE

The arrival of the two buckboards in town, carrying six women and six children, attracted some attention. This was considerably heightened when it was noticed that from the rear of the floor of the first buckboard four pairs of feet encased in boots, were protruding for several inches.

Miriam, driving the leading buckboard, halted for a moment. Ethel Grant, driving the second one, followed suit. Miriam spoke to a man at the forefront of the small group which had collected around them.

'Who's the leading citizen in this town?' she asked.

'That would be Henry Baxter,' said the man. 'If we had a mayor here, he'd be it. He runs the general store along the street there and he owns the boarding-house next door.

He's in the store now.'

Miriam thanked the man, and the two buckboards, followed by the onlookers, moved on and stopped outside the store. Miriam asked the same man if he would ask Mr Baxter to step outside. When the store-keeper appeared, Miriam climbed down from the buckboard and met him on the boardwalk. He was a bearded man of average height, neatly dressed. He stared at the protruding feet of Daley and his men.

'I'm Miriam Farrell,' said Miriam. 'When I was passing through here two years ago the bank had just been robbed by the Daley gang. I guess you remember the day?'

'I sure do,' said Baxter. 'It was a black day for me and Tipawa. Most people's savings were gone and two people were killed. One of them was my wife.'

'In that case,' said Miriam, 'you'll be more than interested to know that we've got the Daley gang in the buckboard there. They had us all prisoner, but we turned the tables on them. If some of the folks here would lift off those tents, you'll be able to see their faces.'

There was mounting excitement as Baxter, with several townspeople helping him, lifted the tents out of the buckboard to reveal the faces of the four outlaws.

'This is the Daley gang all right,' said Baxter. 'I saw them when they raided the bank. How in tarnation did you women manage to capture them?'

'We'll tell you about that later,' said Miriam, 'but first we want to know if you people will guard these men and get the law to come and pick them up?'

'I know a dozen men at least, who'll volunteer for guard duty,' said Baxter, 'and you can take it there'll be no chance at all of the prisoners escaping after what they did to us here. In fact, I reckon I'm going to have to do some fast talking to persuade some of the folks here that a lynching ain't a good idea.

'I'll get a message off right away to the US Marshal at Fort Smith to send some deputies along to take these men in for trial.'

'One other thing,' said Miriam, taking Baxter aside so that she could speak to him privately. 'The husbands of the women with me are homesteaders near Monroe in the Texas Panhandle. It's important that we get a message to them right away. Can you get somebody to ride over there with it?'

'Sure,' said Baxter. 'My son Nat over there takes a ride whenever he gets the chance.'

He called over a young man who was standing in the crowd by the buckboard, looking at the four outlaws.

'Nat,' he said, 'Mrs Farrell here wants to get an urgent message to some home-steaders near Monroe in the Panhandle. I guess that's near fifty miles from here. I want you to take it for her.'

Nat, a pleasant-faced young man, smiled at Miriam.

'Give me twenty minutes, ma'am,' he said, 'and I'll be on my way. What's the message?'

'It's to be given to a man called Jack

Nelson,' she said, 'and not to anybody else. We don't want anybody but him and his friends to know that we're here. You'll find him at one of the six homesteads lined up along the river in the valley close to Monroe.

'Ride in after dawn tomorrow, peaceable-like, and there'll be no danger of you getting shot.'

She went on to give him a detailed description of Jack.

'The message is,' she said, 'that the women have captured the Daley gang and have taken them to Tipawa in Indian Territory, to be handed over to the law. All the women and children are safe, but Hiram Benson was murdered by Daley. The women and children will stay in Tipawa until they hear from the men.'

Nat repeated the message back to her and twenty minutes later he rode fast out of town to the west.

Several willing volunteers dragged Daley and his men out of the buckboard and into an empty shack behind the store. A continuous two-man guard, day and night, was organized.

'Business is pretty slow in the boarding-house just now,' said Baxter, 'and I reckon I can accommodate all you ladies and the children without crowding you in too much. And don't figure on having to spend anything in this town. You're all the guests of the people of Tipawa.'

Grateful, the women drove the buckboard behind the store, unhitched the horses, and led them to the livery stable. Then they took their children into the boarding-house.

Jack and three of the other settlers were taking breakfast at the Lee homestead when Grant, who had been on guard outside, rode up with Nat Baxter and took him into the house.

'This stranger here,' he said, 'has a message for you, Jack. He reckons it's for you and nobody else.'

Jack looked up at Nat, who was inspecting

him closely.

'You're Jack Nelson?' asked Nat.

'That's me,' replied Jack.

'I have a message for you from Mrs Miriam Farrell,' said Nat.

The four men at the table sat bolt upright and waited for him to continue. He passed on Miriam's message, word for word. When he had finished, Jack and the others looked at one another. Relief showed on their faces.

'Well, I'm danged,' said Dixon. 'Four desperados like that taken prisoner by a bunch of females!'

'A special bunch of females, I reckon,' said Jack. 'I just can't wait to hear how they got the better of Daley and his men.'

They listened while Nat described the arrival of the two buckboards in town, with the four trussed outlaws lying in one of them. He told them that until the deputy US marshals arrived, Daley and his men would be guarded so closely that escape would be impossible.

They thanked Nat for bringing the message and offered him some breakfast. While he was eating this, Jack asked him to carry the message back that Mort Lee had recovered from his wound and would be rejoining them later in the day. He also asked Nat to say that the women and children should stay in Tipawa until they got the message that it was safe for them to return.

When he had finished the meal, Nat headed back towards Indian Territory, leaving Jack and the others to discuss the changed situation. First, they agreed that the location of the women and children must be kept a closely-guarded secret. Then they went on to consider what action they might now take.

'I reckon it's possible,' said Jack, 'that Duff doesn't know that the women have escaped, and that he can't rely on Daley and his men for help any more. If that's the case, he won't be expecting any trouble from us, and that gives us a chance to move in on him once more before that freight wagon arrives at the Box D.'

'But what d'you figure on us doing to him now?' asked John Randle.

Jack suggested several possibilities, and one of these was selected. It was decided that the operation would take place during the coming night, with Lee joining in if he wished. But first, they would check whether guards had been posted outside the Box D buildings. Their absence would indicate that the rancher was unaware of the women's escape.

During the afternoon, Jack rode into town to see Ranger and his wife. He told them about the women's escape, asking them to keep the information strictly secret. He said that it was possible that he and the men would soon have to leave the homesteads and find a safe hiding-place not too far away. He asked Ranger if he had any suggestions.

The storekeeper thought for a while, then shook his head. 'Offhand, I can't think of anywhere safe,' he said.

'What about Billy Norton's old place in town?' asked his wife.

'Can't think,' said Ranger, 'that...' He stopped abruptly, then continued. 'Of course!' he exclaimed. 'The underground room!'

He went on to tell Jack about a big derelict house on the edge of town, which had been built by Billy Norton, a close friend of his, soon after the town was founded. Billy and his wife, long-since dead, had raised three children, and they had had a fear of the house being set on fire during an Indian raid.

For this reason, Billy had built in a large underground room, accessible through a concealed trapdoor in the floor.

'I know where that trapdoor is,' said Ranger, 'and I think you'd be safe in there. I doubt if anybody else around here knows about the room, certainly nobody from the Box D.

'And as for your horses, Hal Reynolds, who owns the livery stable just across the street, ain't no friend of Duff's. He's a good man. If I have a word with him, he'll hide your horses away somewhere.'

Jack and the others set off after dark. Lee, keen to join the party after a long spell of inactivity, was with them. They stopped short of the Box D buildings and Jack went ahead on foot. He was back twenty minutes later.

'Not a guard in sight,' he said. 'I guess we can go ahead with the plan.'

Keeping well clear of the ranch buildings, they continued riding east down the valley for several miles until they reached a point where the grazing was lush and cows were sprinkled liberally over the ground. The animals got to their feet as the riders approached.

'We'll spread out and pick up as many cows as we can manage,' said Jack, 'and drive them out of the valley into that rough country to the south. We'll carry on driving them till we've just enough time to get back to the homesteads before daylight.'

The following morning, after their return to the homesteads, it was decided that they would repeat the operation the coming night, if it was evident that the cattle already taken out of the valley had not yet been missed.

They rested during the day, and the following night successfully drove another large bunch of cows out of the valley, after checking that all was quiet around the Box D buildings, and no guard had been posted.

'I think we'll leave it at that,' said Jack, when they had returned to the homesteads. 'What I reckon we should do now is watch out for that freight wagon and see how many men are guarding it. I don't reckon there's any chance of us doing what we did before, but maybe those guards'll be staying on at the Box D, and it'll give us some idea of the number of men we're up against.'

That night Jack and Fisher rode out to a high point overlooking, from a distance, the section of trail where Jack and Grant had destroyed the previous consignment of goods for the Box D. Arriving at dawn, they settled down to watch, through field-glasses, for the arrival of the freight wagon.

It was an hour before noon, on the following day, when Jack first caught sight of it. Following it with the glasses as it came closer, he could see that there were eight riders accompanying the wagon, one of whom looked like Green. When the wagon had moved out of sight, Jack and Fisher rode back to the homesteads, to discuss the situation with the others.

'When Duff finds out about the missing cows,' said Jack, 'and realizes that the women and the Daley gang have vanished, I reckon he's going to come after us with all his men. And that could mean twenty or more men chasing us if the ones with the wagon stay on.

'I reckon that if we want to stay healthy we have no option but to leave the homesteads today, after dark. We'll move into that old house in Monroe that Ranger told me about.'

Taking lamps, weapons, bedrolls and provisions with them, they rode into town after dark, and taking care that they were unobserved by anyone on the street, they left their horses at the livery stable and made their way to the tumbledown Norton dwelling.

Following Ranger's directions, and with the help of an oil lamp, Jack found the cunningly concealed trapdoor in the floor and lifted it up. He climbed down some steps into the space below. The other men followed him. Looking round, they could see that the space was empty, and large enough to accommodate them all without discomfort.

When the freight wagon arrived at the Box D, Willard Duff felt that it was only a matter of time now before he would get rid of the settlers.

But the first blow fell when a ranch hand he had despatched to the eastern end of the range returned in haste some time later. He told the rancher that, at a rough guess, 500 cattle had disappeared from the range. Signs indicated that they had been driven out of the valley one or two days earlier.

Almost apoplectic with rage, Willard Duff sent his son, with three hands, to search for the missing cattle. He suspected that rustlers might be at work, since the settlers would hardly move against him while their women and children were being held by Daley and his men.

The second blow fell when a hand he had despatched to tell Daley that the freight wagon had arrived, returned some hours later, in the evening. The hand told the rancher that the ravine was empty, with no sign, in the vicinity, of the Daley gang, or of the women and children.

Hearing this, Duff immediately suspected that the settlers were responsible for the missing cattle. As for the disappearance of the Daley gang, and the women and children, he couldn't imagine what had happened to them. He was reasonably sure that, after his warning, Nelson and the settlers would have stayed away from the ravine. And he couldn't imagine that half a dozen homesteaders' wives had got the better of Daley and his men. But if the unlikely *had* happened, where were they all now?

He decided to mount an operation the following morning to capture Jack and the settlers.

At first light he left with fifteen hands, including the seven men recruited by Green in Amarillo to guard the freight wagon. They rode first to the homesteads, half expecting an ambush. But they found all the homesteads deserted. Then they rode to Monroe and carried out a fruitless search of the town, during which Jack and the others heard the Box D men moving round on the floor above them. They immediately ceased all conversation and extinguished the lamps until the searchers had left.

Duff and his men then searched the valley and the adjacent area without success, before returning to the ranch about midnight.

The rancher found his son awaiting him to report that the missing cattle had been found well outside the valley, widely scattered over some rough ground. He told his father that he had left the three hands to start on the lengthy process of rounding the cattle up and driving them back to the valley.

Earlier that evening in Monroe, just as the store was about to close, Harker called in for some tobacco. He was the old man paid by Willard Duff to keep the rancher acquainted with any unusual happenings in Monroe, particularly those associated with the homesteaders.

Despite his age, there was nothing wrong with Harker's hearing, and as he walked into the empty store he heard the tail end of a conversation between Ranger and his wife in the living-quarters, just as the storekeeper was opening the connecting door to come into the store. He thought he heard the words 'Norton place' just before Ranger walked through into the store and closed the door behind him.

Thinking nothing of it at the time, Harker purchased his tobacco and walked along to his shack, set back a little way off the main street. He cooked himself a meal, ate it, then sat on a rickety armchair, smoking his pipe.

The words 'Norton place' which he had heard in the store flitted into his mind, and he wondered idly why the Rangers had been talking about it. He knew where the abandoned single-storey building was, although he was not aware of the refuge under the floor. In fact, the building was visible from one of the windows of his shack.

His mind went back to the search, earlier in the day, for Nelson and the homesteaders. Then he sat bolt upright as a thought suddenly struck him. He knew that Ranger and his wife were friendly with the homesteaders, particularly Miriam Farrell.

Could it be that Nelson and the settlers had gone into hiding in the old Norton house after it had been searched by Duff's men earlier in the day? He decided to investigate, knowing that a rich reward would be his if he could deliver Jack Nelson and the others to the rancher.

It was dark outside. Harker left his shack, and keeping off the main street, he walked to the Norton house and stood outside the door, which was half open. He stayed there, listening for a few minutes, but could hear no sound inside. He took off his boots, then slipped silently inside the house, and lighting matches as he went along, he cautiously looked into every room. There was no sign of any occupants.

He stood for a moment in the living-room, disappointed that his suspicions had proved unfounded. Then, just as he was about to move towards the door, he thought that he heard a sound, like a very faint murmur of voices. The sound was intermittent.

He went outside, but the sound was not evident out there. He re-entered the house, and when the faint sound recurred, he lay on the floor, pressed his ear against the floorboards, and listened for a while. He rose to his feet, convinced that the faint sound of voices was coming from underneath the floor. Silently, he left the house, replaced his boots, and returned to his shack.

He sat there for a while, considering his next move. It was clear that he must let Willard Duff know of his suspicions as quickly as possible.

He went to the livery stable for the horse which had been loaned to him by the rancher. He saddled it and rode out on to the street. He did not see the liveryman, Hal Reynolds, but Reynolds, coming into the stable from the rear, caught a glimpse of him as he left. The liveryman wondered where Harker could be going.

At the Box D, Harker announced his arrival to the guard and was taken into the house to see the rancher and his son. They listened to his story with mounting interest.

'I know the house you're talking about,'

said the rancher, when Harker had finished. 'You sure about those voices?'

'Certain,' replied Harker.

'There could be a space under the floor,' said Willard Duff. 'Some of the older houses were built like that.'

He turned to his son.

'Get eight men together, Brad,' he said. 'Then you and me'll ride into town with them and take a good look at the Norton house.'

Harker rode into town before them, stabled his horse, then went to his shack. Reynolds saw him come in to the stable.

The men from the Box D, carrying some oil lamps with them, kept off the main street, riding along the backs of the buildings, and dismounted a little way from the Norton house. They approached it silently on foot, then stopped outside. Brad Duff took off his boots and tiptoed into the house alone.

When he came out fifteen minutes later, he whispered to his father.

'Harker was right,' he said. 'It ain't easy to hear, but I reckon there's at least two men under that floor.'

'We'll go in and find the trapdoor,' said Willard Duff. 'Three men stay outside, in case there's another way out.'

Underneath the floor, Jack and his companions turned the lamps down and listened with mounting concern as they heard the sounds of a number of people walking round on the floor above.

It took Duff and his men quite some time to find the trapdoor. It was cunningly concealed in what appeared to be a large chest, standing on the floor in a corner of the living-room. The chest in fact, had no bottom, and stood over the trapdoor, which was covered with material of some kind. A piece of stout cord was attached to the door to enable it to be pulled open.

The two Duffs and the Box D hands stood around the chest, a little way back from it, all holding six-guns in their hands. Brad Duff leaned forward, grasped the cord, and slowly pulled the trapdoor open until it rested against the end of the chest. They heard no sound from below.

Willard Duff shouted down through the aperture in the floor.

'We know you're down there, Nelson,' he said. 'You ain't got a chance against the ten of us up here. Leave your weapons down there and come out. If you don't make your minds up soon, I've got a stick of dynamite here with a short fuse cord that I'm going to drop in on you.'

Jack guessed that the rancher was bluffing, but it made no difference. They were in a hopeless situation in any case. He dropped his six-gun on the floor and climbed out through the aperture. His companions followed suit. As they emerged they were searched for weapons and their hands were bound.

Willard Duff spoke to Jack.

'You've caused me a heap of trouble, Nelson,' he said, 'and I'm going to make you sorry that you stayed on in the valley to help these settlers.'

He turned to Brad.

'We'll gag them,' he said, 'then take them to the Box D. They can ride double with six of the hands. It ain't that far.'

They rode quietly out of town, avoiding the main street, and as far as Duff was aware, nobody in town had witnessed the capture of Jack and the settlers. It was not until later in the evening that Ranger, who went along to discuss the situation with Jack, found that they had vanished.

With the help of a lamp he had taken with him he examined the ground outside the house. There were signs that a number of horses had been moving around there quite recently and he feared that Jack and the others had been captured by Duff's men and had been taken to the Box D. He decided to ride to Tipawa immediately, to tell Miriam and the other women of the latest developments.

When the Duffs and the Box D hands arrived at the ranch buildings with their prisoners, the rancher spoke to his son.

'Six is too many to keep in the house,' he said. 'Better put them in the barn.'

Lamps were lit inside the barn and the prisoners were left there, sitting against a wall, with their hands and feet tied. Two men were stationed inside the barn to guard them. All hands were told that the capture of the prisoners was to remain a secret known only to those at the Box D and Harker in town.

Inside the ranch house the rancher discussed the situation with his son.

'Those prisoners,' he said, 'just don't seem to want to listen to reason. We've got to finish them off for good without anybody outside knowing for certain we had anything to do with it. We've got to fix it so's they vanish without trace. I did think of dropping them in that stretch of quicksand along the river, but I ain't sure they'd vanish for good. You got any ideas?'

'Maybe I have,' replied Brad. 'When we were looking outside the valley the other day for those missing cattle, I came across a cave in the wall of a small canyon. I noticed there was an overhang above the entrance.

'What if we leave Nelson and the others in that cave and bring the overhang down with a few sticks of dynamite? They'd be buried alive. And nobody'd ever find them in there.'

'That's a good idea,' said Willard Duff. 'We'll do it ourselves, you and me. And we'll take Blaney along. I know he won't talk, and he knows more about explosives than anybody else on the ranch. As for the others, we'll tell them that we're taking the prisoners well out of the valley, then freeing them.'

'Right,' said Brad, 'but I've just remembered that we've run out of dynamite. I'll get some tomorrow.'

But when he rode into town the following morning, he found there was none available. However, some was expected by freight wagon the same evening. He returned to the ranch and told his father that he would go back to Monroe later in the day to pick up the dynamite.

'We'll keep the prisoners in the barn until the dynamite arrives,' said the rancher, 'with two men guarding them all the time.'

Inside the barn, the prisoners had a chance to talk together when the guards stood smoking outside the open door.

'Can't think how Duff got the idea we were hiding under that floor,' said Jack. 'I'm sure it weren't due to Ranger. We've got a big problem now. Duff's guarding us pretty closely. It ain't likely we're going to be able to escape.'

'What d'you reckon he means to do with us?' asked Lee.

'Maybe escort us out of the valley, like he said he would,' Jack replied, 'but I wouldn't bank on it. You can tell he's pretty riled over all the trouble we've given him. Maybe he's got something else in store for us.'

TEN

When Ranger arrived in Tipawa with the news of the disappearance of Jack and the others, the women were dismayed and apprehensive. They discussed the situation, sitting in a room in the boarding-house, while Ranger had a meal.

'I reckon that Duff's holding them,' said Miriam. 'I think that we've got to try and help them. How do the rest of you feel?'

From the replies, it was clear that all the other women agreed, and when Ranger came in they told him that they intended to go into hiding somewhere near Monroe and try to find out where Jack and the other men were being held. She said they would contact him when they arrived. Ranger then departed for Monroe.

Miriam went to see Henry Baxter and

explained the situation to him.

'We've all decided to ride into the Pan-handle,' she said, 'and go into hiding some-where near Monroe. But you can see the problem we have. We can't take the children with us. D'you reckon we could leave them in Tipawa for a spell?'

'Of course,' Baxter replied, 'that is, if you're set on leaving. You could be heading into real danger.'

'We're sure,' said Miriam. 'We've talked about it and our minds are made up.'

'Right,' said Baxter, 'in that case I can promise you that after what you've done there's plenty of married couples around here who'll be happy to take your children in for a spell. You can leave it to me to fix that.

'And another thing I'm going to do is fit you all out with proper riding clothes. I've got plenty in the store.'

Ignoring their protests, he continued. 'I'll loan you a couple more horses and you can carry the weapons you took from the Daley gang, together with any more you might need. I reckon that Duff would be shaking in his boots if he knew you ladies were coming after him.

'And there's something I have to tell you,' he went on, 'I happen to know there's a big reward'll come to you for the capture of the Daley gang. I'm sure you'll all find that useful when it comes. When d'you figure on leaving?'

'At daylight tomorrow,' Miriam replied.

'What I'd like you to do now,' said Baxter, 'is come along with me to see an old friend of mine, called Tex Lander. I'll leave you with him while I go round finding places for your children. Tex was a town marshal till he retired, and some folks reckoned he had no equal as a gunfighter. Maybe he can give you some quick tips about gun-handling that'll come in useful.'

They followed him to a small shack along the street, and waited outside while he went in. A few minutes later, he beckoned them inside and introduced them to Lander, who was standing by his armchair. Then he left.

Lander was a tall, thin man in his seventies, slightly stooped, with a moustache that drooped down past the corners of his mouth. He suffered from rheumatism, and one of his ears had been slightly disfigured by a passing bullet. He eyed the women quizzically.

'Ladies,' he said. 'Like you see, I'm a bit short of furniture in here, so we'll have to do this standing up. I heard about you bringing the Daley gang in, which is why I'm glad to help you if I can.'

'We appreciate it,' said Miriam.

'We can only cover the basics now,' said Lander. 'It takes a long time, and a lot of practice to turn out an expert gunfighter, even if he has a natural talent for the job. Watch me closely.'

He took out a well-worn gunbelt and a Colt .45 single-action revolver from a drawer. He buckled on the gunbelt, then took the gun to pieces to show them the working parts. They watched him with close attention.

He reassembled the gun and slipped it into the holster. He showed them how to adjust the belt so that the holster rested snugly on the hip at the right height for the hand to grasp the gun handle for a smooth draw.

Then he showed them how to draw the gun, raising the muzzle as it left the holster, how to cock it, using the thumb over the hammer; and how to point it and fire. He repeated the operation a number of times.

'Maybe you've done this all before,' he said, when he had finished. 'What I'm doing is to show you the *right* way of doing it. And there's one important thing to remember: don't hurry things too much, or you'll likely miss the target. And get as much target practice in as you can.'

He put the revolver and gunbelt back in the drawer and lifted a Winchester .44 rifle off the wall. He showed them how to load and reload it, aim and fire. He repeated the operation several times.

'I reckon that's the best I can do in the

time we've got, ladies,' he said, 'and whatever it is you're going to do, I sure hope you manage to pull it off.'

They thanked the old lawman and returned to the boarding-house.

'When we ride into the Panhandle tomorrow,' said Miriam, 'I reckon the best place to hide will be in the ravine where Daley captured us. We'll aim to arrive there around dawn. There ain't no reason just now for Duff to have men searching that area. And while we're on the way there, we'll take some time off for target practice.'

Half an hour later Baxter came in to say that he had found temporary homes for all the children, and that they would be able to attend the school in town while their mothers were away. Later, he brought in the clothing, weapons and ammunition that he had promised, along with some provisions.

He said the horses and bedrolls would be ready for them in the morning and that he would provide a smaller mount for Debbie Randle, who barely topped five feet.

After saying goodbye to the children, they left soon after dawn the following morning. Each of them was dressed in pants, shirt and vest. Each was wearing cowboy boots and a Texas hat. The townspeople assembled to see them off.

On the day before the women left Tipawa, Brad Duff picked the dynamite up in town and took it out to the ranch. His father decided that the two of them, with Blaney, would take the prisoners out to the cave the following morning.

The rancher got up early and as he was finishing breakfast he saw, through the ranch house window, a salesman called Laker riding towards the house. Laker worked for a company which sold general ranch supplies and machinery, and Duff had dealt with him in the past.

He went out to meet Laker, telling him brusquely that he had no business for him at that time. Disappointed, Laker turned to leave, intending to ride on to a big ranch to the north. Then he paused.

'Did you hear about the Daley gang?' asked the rancher.

'No,' replied Duff. 'What about them?'

'Damndest thing I ever heard of,' replied Laker. 'They were captured by six settlers' wives somewhere in the Panhandle and taken to Tipawa in Indian Territory for the law to collect.

'I was in Tipawa early yesterday and the story I heard was that those women were getting ready to ride off to the Panhandle to find their husbands, who'd gone missing. They were dressed in cowboy clothes, and all wearing guns. The folks in Tipawa were going to look after their children while they were away.'

Duff got rid of the salesman, calling out after him as he left that it was good news about the Daley gang. Then he sent for two of his men. One of them was Jackson, who had been with him for some time. The other was Barclay, who had arrived with the freight wagon. Duff stood, immersed in thought, until they arrived. Then he spoke to Jackson.

'You know the homesteader Farrell's boy?' he asked.

'Sure,' replied Jackson. 'About ten years old, with fair hair. Called Danny, I think.'

'Good,' said Duff. 'I happen to know that he's in Tipawa in Indian Territory with the children of the other homesteaders. Their mothers have left them there, and the townspeople are looking after them.

'I want you two to ride off now and pick up Danny Farrell when nobody's looking and bring him back here. No need to harm him. And get back here as quickly as you can. There'll be a bonus for you when you've done the job.'

After watching the two hands leave, the rancher and his son, together with Blaney, set off with the prisoners. They rode in single file, with Willard Duff in the lead, his son behind him, trailing the prisoners' horses, and Blaney bringing up the rear. The prisoners' hands were tied in front of them.

When they reached the canyon, they stopped outside the cave and Brad Duff ordered the prisoners to dismount and go inside. He followed them in and ordered them to sit on the floor while he stood guard over them. The cave was roughly circular, about thirteen feet in diameter. The lowest point on the ceiling was about seven feet from the floor.

Blaney looked inside the cave, then at the canyon wall above the cave entrance. Then he rode out of the canyon and up to the top of the wall above the cave entrance, where he closely studied the ground.

When he returned to the rancher, standing outside the cave out of earshot of the prisoners, he told him that he had examined the ground above, and that a few sticks of dynamite, dropped into some of the deep cracks he had found, would bring enough rock and soil down to block the cave entrance for good.

'Good,' said the rancher. 'First, we'll bind the prisoners so tight they won't be able to move inside there. Bring that rope along.'

They went inside the cave, and while the rancher held a gun on the prisoners, his son and Blaney bound each of them so effectively that, lying on their backs at the rear of the cave, they had not the slightest chance of freeing themselves by their own efforts. Blaney went outside.

The rancher stood looking down on them with grim satisfaction for a while, before he spoke.

'This is the end of the road for you men,' he said. 'You've caused me a heap of trouble, but you were fools to think you could get away with it. Right now, my hand Blaney's on his way to place some dynamite on top of the canyon wall over this cave. When that dynamite goes off you men are going to be sealed up inside here for good, and it don't bother me none that maybe it'll take you a long time to die.'

'You're sick, Duff,' said Jack, 'and a fool as well. You're bound to be found out. The women will see to that.'

'Not a chance,' said the rancher. 'Nobody saw us take you prisoner and nobody saw us bring you here. And your bodies will never be found. Suspicion is all there'll be, nothing else.'

The two Duffs walked out of the cave and the prisoners heard the rancher shouting to Blaney at the top of the canyon wall.

'It looks like this is the end for us,' said Jack. 'I'm sure sorry I got you men into this situation.'

'It was our own decision,' said Grant. 'It ain't your fault. I reckon we were doing pretty good up to now. At least the women and children are safe.'

The other men, their faces showing the strain they were under, nodded agreement.

It was some time before they heard the rancher shouting to Blaney again. Then, after a further five minutes' silence, the explosions came. Suddenly, the light coming through the cave entrance was blotted out as a mass of rock fragments and earth fell from above and completely blocked the cave entrance.

Inside the cave, the six bound men closed their eyes and choked as they were enveloped in a thick cloud of dust. It was some time before this settled and the coughing ceased. Then there was an eerie silence, broken only by an occasional slight movement in the rubble which was blocking them in.

Some debris had come into the cave, and all the men had been struck by pieces of rock. But they were not buried, and although three of them were bleeding and bruised, it appeared that nobody was badly injured. They lay in pitch blackness, barely able to move because of the ropes which were binding them so tightly, and wondering how long they would survive.

In vain, Jack looked upwards to see if there was the faintest chink of light to indicate that some fresh air would find its way inside to prevent their deaths from lack of oxygen. But even if air *was* coming in, he knew that it would only postpone their deaths. The lack of food and water would eventually take its toll.

Outside the cave, the two Duffs and Blaney waited until the dust had settled. Then they closely inspected the mound of debris covering the cave entrance.

'That should do the trick,' said the rancher. 'I think we can say that we've seen the last of Nelson and his friends. Now we can deal with the women.'

Taking the six extra horses with them, they headed for the Box D.

The women, after camping out overnight, rode into the ravine at daybreak and posted a lookout to watch for approaching riders. They had decided that one of them would ride into Monroe after dark to contact Ranger and see if there was any news about the whereabouts of Jack and the others.

A little before noon, May Dixon, who was on lookout, ran down to say that a man was approaching on a mule, trailing a burro behind him.

'A prospector, for sure,' she said.

'We'll let him ride in here, if that's what he's aiming to do,' said Miriam. 'I suppose there's just a chance he might give us some useful information.'

Abe Leary hesitated as he approached the ravine, then turned the mule to head for the entrance. Once inside, he pulled up sharp and stared at the six armed women standing by an old shack at the side of the ravine. They walked towards Leary and stopped in front of him. He studied them closely. Despite the weapons they were wearing he didn't feel unduly intimidated.

'Ladies,' he said, 'this is a real treat for me. It ain't often I rides into a place like this, in the middle of nowhere, and finds six women, as good-looking as you, waiting to say "Howdy". In fact, I don't recollect it ever happening to me before.'

Miriam smiled at him. 'We're having a meal in a few minutes,' she said. 'Happen you'd like to join us?'

With as much alacrity as his ageing joints

would allow, the prospector dismounted.

'I'm obliged,' he said. 'The name's Leary, Abe Leary.'

Miriam introduced herself and the other women, who then busied themselves over the preparation of the meal. May Dixon returned to the lookout position.

Leary spotted the cross at the head of the grave of Hiram Benson, murdered in the ravine by Daley. He wandered over to it and bent down to read the name which was roughly marked on it.

'Well, I'm danged!' he said, and walked over to Miriam.

'That grave over there,' he said, 'd'you happen to know anything about the man inside it?'

'I do,' replied Miriam. 'He was a friend of ours, murdered by an outlaw called Daley.'

'Was he a prospector like myself?' asked Leary.

'Yes, he was,' replied Miriam.

'Then he was an old partner of mine,' said Leary. 'We were together in the '49 gold rush in California, and split up about eight years later. I often wondered what happened to Hiram.'

'We can tell you what happened to him *here*,' said Miriam, 'but we'd better leave it till after we've eaten.'

The old prospector enjoyed a more appetizing meal than he had had for some time, and he enjoyed the company. When the meal was over the women told him how they had been captured in the ravine by the Daley gang, who had killed his old partner Hiram Benson; and how they had got the better of the outlaws and had handed them over to the law in Tipawa.

'All I can say, ladies,' said Leary, 'is that I sure am glad you've got nothing against me. I ain't meaning to pry, but what you've told me up to now don't explain what you're doing here.'

'It's our menfolk,' said May Dixon, the strain showing on her face. 'Six of them altogether. They've vanished. And we're here to find them. We think that Duff has

172

them, but we ain't got no proof of that. We're all worried sick about them.'

'We've got a friend in Monroe,' said Miriam. 'One of us is riding in there after dark, to see if he knows where they are.'

Leary scratched his head for a moment, then spoke.

'Six men, you say? By Jiminy! They could be the ones you're talking about.'

The women crowded around him.

'What d'you mean?' asked Miriam.

'Well,' replied Leary, 'yesterday morning I was taking a rest on some high ground north of the valley and east of here, when I spotted nine riders heading north in single file. It sort of looked like six of the riders had their hands tied and were being led by one of the other three. I kept my head down, because I've found out that wandering around like I do, it's wise for a man to mind his own business.'

'What were the prisoners like?' asked Ethel Grant, urgently.

'I weren't all that close,' said Leary, 'but I

did notice that one of them was a big man, well over six feet, I'd say.'

'Jim!' exclaimed Ethel Grant.

'And another,' Leary continued, 'was probably only a shade over five feet.'

'That's John!' said Debbie Randle.

'What about the three men with the prisoners?' asked Miriam.

'The two in front were both heavy-built,' Leary replied. 'A bit on the fat side, I'd say.'

'The Duffs, for sure,' said Miriam. 'You say they were heading north, Mr Leary?'

'For as long as I could see them,' Leary replied, 'but they soon passed out of sight. Then a funny thing happened. About forty minutes after they disappeared, when I had moved off and was heading in this direction, I heard explosions from the area they'd been heading into, and I saw a dust-cloud in the sky.

'Like I said before, I learnt a long time ago that being nosy ain't a good idea, so I didn't ride over to see what was happening.'

'Will you take us to the place where you

saw those riders?' asked Miriam. 'Maybe we can get on the trail of our menfolk. And we'd like to know just what those explosions were about.'

'Sure,' replied Leary. 'You want to go right now?'

'Please,' replied Miriam. 'The sooner, the better.'

Inside the cave, Jack and the others had spent a night of extreme discomfort in the darkness. None of them had been able to loosen the ropes which were binding them so tightly. They were all suffering from the immobility this situation produced.

Unable to do anything to help themselves, they discussed their desperate situation only sporadically. After a long silence, Grant spoke.

'I'm wondering,' he said, 'if there's any chance of the women finding us here?'

'I've got to say,' said Jack, not wishing to raise any false hopes, 'that I reckon the chance of that happening is pretty slim. On the other hand, look what they did to Daley and the others. Who would have expected that?'

He and his companions were finding it more and more difficult to breathe as the long hours dragged by.

ELEVEN

It was shortly after three o'clock when the women, led by Leary on his mule, reached the place from which he had seen the nine riders the previous day. They paused, then he led them to the point at which the riders had disappeared from view.

'Let me ride ahead a little,' said the prospector. 'Following tracks of any sort has always been a hobby of mine. I reckon it ain't going to be hard to follow these.'

He led the women northward, glancing down at the tracks as he went along. A mile further on, they led into a small canyon. Leary halted inside the canyon and dismounted. The women followed suit.

The prospector walked up to a big pile of debris standing against the wall of the canyon and looked upwards. He mounted his mule.

'Stay here,' he said to the women. 'I've got to take a look at the top of the canyon wall. I'll be back soon.'

Impatiently, they awaited his return. When he rode back twenty minutes later he told them that he had seen horse tracks above and that there was evidence that dynamite had been used to bring down part of the canyon wall.

'I was in this canyon a week ago,' he said, 'and I can tell you there's a cave behind that pile of rock and earth you see there. I spent a night in there.'

'I'm getting a bad feeling about this place,' said Miriam.

The other women were looking at one another with mounting concern.

'I know what you're thinking,' said Leary. 'But we've got to be sure. Give me another fifteen minutes.'

He rode out of the canyon and followed some horse tracks leading south and angling away slightly from the ones they had followed to the canyon earlier. He was sure they had been made by the same horses.

On a clear soft stretch of ground he dismounted and studied the tracks closely for several minutes. Then he returned to the women.

'It's clear,' he said, 'that the nine horses that were ridden in here left later and headed south, but not in single file. And I could tell from the depth of the tracks that six of them weren't carrying riders.'

'So Duff put our men in the cave and blocked the entrance by using dynamite?' said Miriam, 'and they've been there well over twenty-four hours?' Her voice was shaking.

'It sure looks that way,' said Leary.

'We've got to get them out,' said May Dixon, frantically, and the women ran up to the mass of debris blocking the cave entrance.

'Hold on a minute!' shouted Leary. 'This has to be done right, or you'll waste a lot of time. What we need to do is make a hole through this pile near the top of the cave entrance.'

He showed them where to pull out pieces of rock before dropping them to the ground. All the women climbed on to the pile, and they worked in feverish haste, with bare hands, praying that the entombed men were still alive.

When darkness came, Leary took a lamp from his burro and lit it. One of the women held it while the others worked on, with bleeding and aching hands and arms.

It was over four hours before Debbie Randle, trying to pull a piece of rock out from the back of the large hole they had created, felt it slip from her grasp and fall down inside the cave.

She told the others and they redoubled their efforts until they had formed a hole about fifteen inches in diameter, right through into the cave. Then Miriam called for silence, poked her head through the hole, and called out.

'Anybody there?' she shouted.

The men inside the cave, gasping for breath, had been aware for a while that somebody was trying to reach them. Hearing Miriam's call they all tried to shout back, but all that their tortured lungs could produce was a concerted croaking sound.

It was enough for Miriam.

'They're alive!' she shouted, and the women continued their efforts until there was a hole large enough for the men to pass through.

Ethel Grant and Miriam, taking the lamp with them, passed through the hole and slid down to the floor of the cave. Looking at the six bound men, they were greatly relieved to see that all were alive.

Miriam passed the good news outside and called for a knife. She cut the ropes around the six men.

'That's better,' wheezed Jack, 'but it's going to be a while before we can climb out through that hole.'

'We've got some rope out there,' said Miriam. 'We'll pull you out. The sooner we get you all into the fresh air, the better.'

When the men were all outside, Leary got a fire going, and the homesteaders' wives attended to their husbands' cuts and bruises, then to their own hands and arms. Miriam attended to Jack, bathing a bad cut on the side of his head.

'I reckon you just got here in the nick of time,' he said. 'Can't think how you found out where we were.'

'It's a long story,' she said, 'and it can wait while we get some food and drink into you. We've brought plenty with us.'

Later on, both sides told their stories, and it was decided that they might as well stay where they were for the time being, with a lookout posted on top of the canyon wall as a precaution. There seemed to be no reason why Duff or any of his men would return to the canyon in the near future. With the exception of the lookout, they all rested until dawn.

When daylight came, the men were intrigued when they had a clear view of the women in their riding outfits, and wearing gunbelts.

'It's a frightening sight,' joked big Jim Grant. 'If Willard Duff could see you women now, he'd be wishing he'd never tangled with us homesteaders.'

'Don't forget,' said Jack, 'that these ladies captured the Daley gang, which is something the law has never been able to do.'

'That's right,' said Miriam, 'and from now on we ain't going to hide away in some ravine while you men do the fighting. We'll do it side by side.'

Later on, Jack decided that he would ride into Monroe after dark to see Ranger and pick up the six horses which had been left at the livery stable. He would also ask the storekeeper for some weapons and ammuntion. In the meantime, they would fill up the escape hole through the debris at the cave entrance, so that there was no indication that they had managed to escape.

At nine o'clock on the morning of the day

Abe Leary met the settlers' wives in the ravine, the two Box D hands Jackson and Barclay rode into Tipawa and headed for the saloon. It was not long before the talkative barkeep, who introduced himself as Ben Ridley, had given them the full story of the arrival of the Daley gang with their captors.

'The women left town yesterday,' he said. 'Something to do with finding their menfolk. They left the children here.'

'The townsfolk are looking after them?' asked Jackson.

'That's right,' said the barkeep. 'As a matter of fact, one of them, called Danny Farrell, is staying with me and my wife.'

Jackson and Barclay looked at one another.

'You live in the saloon?' asked Barclay.

'Not likely,' said the barkeep. 'Couldn't stand the noise and the smell of liquor all the time. We have a little house on the south edge of town. All painted white. You can't miss it. I can tell you, I spent a lot of time licking that place into shape.'

'You got a school here?' asked Jackson.

'Sure,' replied the bartender. 'It's just past the boarding-house, on the other side of the street. We're darned lucky to have it. It's open nine-thirty to three every day, except Saturdays and Sundays.'

'You sure are lucky,' said Barclay.

The two men left the saloon and walked along the boardwalk until they reached a point opposite the school. The pupils were beginning to arrive.

Then Jackson saw Danny Farrell. He quickly turned his back to the boy to avoid recognition.

'That's him,' he said to his companion, 'the boy with fair hair, just passing the boarding-house.'

'I see him,' said Barclay. 'When do we take him?'

'When he comes out of school, I reckon,' Jackson replied. 'Let's go and take a look at the barkeep's house. Maybe we can pick him up near there. We'd never take him in the middle of town without being spotted.'

They soon located the Ridley house, distinctive in its coat of white paint, and standing alone. Just before they reached it, they came to a shack which appeared to be unoccupied and in a poor state of repair. They had a look inside, then came out and walked round to look at the back.

They returned to the centre of town, and taking a meal at the restaurant at midday, they idled around till twenty to three, then rode to the shack next to the barkeep's house and tethered their horses behind it. Jackson went inside.

Barclay walked back towards the centre of town for fifty yards, then waited. It was not long before he saw Danny walking in his direction, on the other side of the street. As the boy drew level, Barclay crossed over and spoke to him.

'Maybe you can help me, son,' he said. 'I'm looking for the Ridley house.'

'I'm staying there myself, mister,' said Danny. 'Come along, and I'll show you.'

Just as they reached the shack, walking side by side, Barclay looked around. There was no one in sight. He grabbed Danny's arms and bundled the boy through the door into the shack, where Jackson was waiting to clamp his hand over Danny's mouth.

The boy struggled frantically as he recognized Jackson, but the two men quickly had him gagged, and bound so tightly that he could barely move. Then they pulled a sack down over his head, and another up over his feet, and tied them firmly in place.

First checking that there was nobody in the vicinity, they carried Danny outside and slung him across the saddle of Jackson's horse. Then they rode slowly out of town, with Jackson seated behind the saddle. A mile out of town they released Danny and continued on towards the Box D, with Danny alternatively riding with Jackson, then Barclay. It was some time before it was realized, in Tipawa, that Danny was missing.

They arrived at the Box D in the afternoon of the following day. The two men reported to Willard Duff that the women had left Tipawa. He gave orders that the scared boy be held in one of the bedrooms in the house, with a continuous guard in the room, relieved every four hours.

The rancher then rode into Monroe to see Ranger, the storekeeper. He had with him a small exercise book which Danny had been carrying when he was captured. When he requested a private conversation with Ranger, the storekeeper took him through into the living quarters, while his wife attended to the customers in the store.

'I know,' said Duff, 'that you're friendly with the settlers, 'specially the Farrells, and I'm pretty sure in my own mind that you're in contact with them.

'I want you to let them know that I'm set on getting them all out of this valley for good. Tell them I'm holding young Danny Farrell out at the ranch, but he'll come to no harm if they all ride to the Box D and hand over their weapons. When they get here, I'll tell them what they've got to do next.'

He handed Danny's exercise book over to Ranger.

'Show them this,' he said, 'in case they doubt that I've got the boy.'

Ranger couldn't control his anger over the kidnapping of Danny, and Duff's ultimatum.

'I didn't think,' he said, 'that even you, Duff, would sink so low as to threaten harm to a young boy to get your own greedy way.'

Duff glared at the storekeeper. 'You'd better mind your tongue, Ranger,' he said, 'or you can start worrying about your own skin.'

'I'll pass on the message as soon as I can,' said Ranger. 'When that'll be, I don't know. I've got no idea where they are just now.'

'Make it quick,' said Duff. 'I ain't a patient man.'

When Duff had gone, Ranger considered the quandary he was in. He had no idea of the whereabouts of any of the homesteaders, men or women, yet it was vital to let them know about Danny as soon as possible.

Remembering Miriam's promise to contact him when they arrived in the area, he decided that all he could do was to wait until that happened. In the absence of any contact with Jack and the other men since they disappeared from the Norton house, he feared that the worst might have happened to them.

Sitting with his wife in the living-quarters, late in the evening, he heard a knock on the door. It was with considerable relief, when he opened it, that he saw Jack standing outside. Quickly, he ushered him in.

'We'd just about given you up for good,' he said. 'We figured that maybe Duff had got rid of all six of you.'

'It was a mighty close call,' said Jack, and proceeded to tell Ranger and his wife of the events subsequent to their capture by Duff and his men at the Norton house.

'I'm sure glad to hear,' Ranger said, when Jack had finished, 'that you and the women have joined up. But I have some bad news for you. Duff was in here earlier. He's holding young Danny Farrell at the ranch. I reckon he sent men to capture him at Tipawa. He asked me to pass on a message.'

Ranger handed over Danny's exercise book and repeated to Jack the ultimatum issued by Duff.

'I told him,' he said, 'that I wasn't sure when I'd be able to deliver the message.'

'This *is* bad news,' said Jack, 'and it's really going to upset the women. We've got to try and rescue Danny, and the only advantage we have is that Duff doesn't know that we men are still alive. We've got to keep it that way as long as we can.

'We'll need those six horses that we left at the livery stable, and we need weapons and ammunition for the men.'

'I'll bring the horses over before you leave,' said Ranger, 'and I can supply the weapons and ammunition.'

'We couldn't have managed without your help,' said Jack. 'Everybody's mighty grateful. And all this stuff you're supplying us with, it'll be paid for when things get back to normal.'

'I know that,' said Ranger. 'I ain't worried on that score. There's one other thing,' he went on. 'I've been wondering how Duff came to know you were at the Norton place. Well, Hal Reynolds, the liveryman, told me that on the evening that you disappeared, he saw an old-timer called Harker, who lives in town, pick up his horse and ride off. He wondered where he could be going. Judging by the time he brought his horse back, he could've ridden to the Box D and back. And on top of that, he's been seen talking to Box D hands pretty regular.'

'Looks like he may be passing information on to Duff, then,' said Jack.

'I'm sure of it,' said Ranger. 'He knows pretty well everything that's going on around town. Sits out on his porch every morning without fail from around nine till midday, and sometimes in the afternoon, keeping an eye on all the action. I reckon that, somehow, he must have found out that you men were in the Norton house, and that he passed the information on to Duff.'

Ranger and Jack went into the store and selected the necessary weapons and ammunition, together with some provisions. Then Ranger went to the livery stable for the six horses. Making sure he was unobserved, he led them round to the back of the store.

Jack gave him the location of the canyon where he and the settlers were now hiding, and said that they would be in contact with him if necessary.

Leaving the store, Jack walked along to the doctor's house and knocked on the door. Shannon, looking surprised to see him, let him in.

'I heard you were in trouble,' he said.

'We were,' said Jack. 'Deep trouble, but we had a stroke of luck. I'm here because we think that young Danny Farrell's being held prisoner at the Box D, most likely in the ranch house. I know what the outside looks like, but I've never been inside. I wonder if you'd been inside yourself.'

'I have,' Shannon replied. 'I went to see Willard Duff once, when he was ill.'

He pencilled a rough sketch of the layout of the two floors on a sheet of paper. 'As I recollect,' he said, 'there were three bedrooms upstairs, but there may have been four.'

'Many thanks for the information, doc,' said Jack. 'I reckon it's going to be mighty useful.'

Jack left town, leading six horses behind him and riding in the shadows of the buildings lining the street. When he arrived at the canyon his news was received with general dismay. Miriam, naturally, was particularly distressed.

'Duff wouldn't harm a young boy, would he?' she asked Jack.

'I don't think,' said Jack, 'that he'll do anything like that until he's sure that Ranger's managed to pass on his message. So that gives us a few days to rescue Danny.

'Don't forget that Duff thinks that me and

the other men are dead. So that gives us an advantage over him. It's clear we've got some careful planning to do. We've all got to get our heads together.

'It seems to me that we have two jobs to do. First, we've got to free Danny as soon as we can. Then we've got to hand over to the law the two Duffs and Blaney, and whoever it was that kidnapped Danny, as well as the man who killed your husband, if we can find out who that is.

'Meanwhile, Miriam, try not to worry too much about Danny. He's a tough little youngster. He'll be all right till we set him free. I'm going to try and work out a plan now to do just that.'

He sat on the ground and concentrated his mind on the problem. Sometime later, he called everyone together, including Leary.

'Mr Leary,' he said, 'it's due to you that we men are still alive to carry on the fight with Duff. Now there's something else you could do to help us get Danny back. Something that wouldn't carry any risk to yourself. Are you willing to give it a try?'

'I sure am,' replied Leary. 'Just tell me what you want me to do. It ain't often I gets the chance to take part in an operation like this.'

'Thanks,' said Jack. 'Just sit down with all of us and we'll discuss the plan.'

He told them how he thought they might first rescue Danny, then deal with Duff and his men. His plan was discussed and modified, but only slightly.

'I think we can start on the plan after we've had a few hours' sleep,' said Jack. 'We can all ride off together.'

Later on, while it was still dark, they all rode out of the canyon, after removing all signs of their presence there. Parting company with the women, who were all wearing weapons and their cowboy clothing, the men headed for some high ground which bordered the valley towards the eastern end of the Box D range.

They stopped there and dismounted, out of sight of anybody down in the valley below. Jack and Leary crawled forward and looked down into the valley, which was well dotted with grazing cows. There were no signs of any Box D cowboys.

'I'm figuring,' said Jack, 'that Duff has got around to looking after his cattle properly again after all that trouble we gave him. He knows they've got to be watched pretty close to keep them healthy. Which is why I'm hoping to see a cowboy, or maybe more than one, riding out here soon.'

He was not disappointed. Half an hour later they saw a lone rider, a Box D hand called Brady, approaching slowly from the west. Brady was weaving slowly through the herd, pausing frequently to look at individual cows.

'I reckon it's time now,' said Jack, 'for me and the other men to leave. Give us twenty minutes, then you can go into the valley and have your chat with the cowboy down there.'

Jack and the settlers, keeping out of sight of Brady, rode east for a while, then down into the valley and over to the river. Taking advantage of the cover afforded by the trees fringing the river, they reached a small grove of trees about sixty yards from the ranch house, without being observed. They stopped and tethered the horses. Then they waited and watched.

TWELVE

Twenty minutes after Jack and the others had left him, Leary rode his mule down into the valley, trailing his burro behind him. He set his course to pass close to Brady, still slowly weaving his way through the herd. Brady saw Leary approaching him and he rode up to the prospector.

'Howdy,' said Leary. 'You having trouble with these cows?'

'It's the darned blowflies,' said Brady, glad of a chance to talk with somebody. 'There's a lot of them around just now. I'm going to have to go for some help. We need to daub the sores with carbolic acid and axle grease. That generally does the trick.'

They chatted for a while about cattle-raising and prospecting in general, then Leary took his leave of the cowboy. He had only gone a few paces when he stopped, and turned.

'I was meaning to ask you,' he said to Brady, 'what a bunch of six females, dressed like cowboys and all wearing guns, would be doing in these parts?'

Brady was all attention.

'Where did you see them?' he asked.

'There's a deep basin on some high ground about three miles due north of this valley,' replied Leary. 'I was watching the women from cover and I don't reckon they saw me. Looked like they were camping there. They had a fire going, with a cooking pot hanging over it.'

'I know that basin,' said Brady. 'Reckon I'll have to leave you now.'

'So long,' said Leary, and rode on in the same direction he had been taking when he approached the cowhand. But when he was out of sight of Brady he altered course and headed for the ravine where he had first met the women.

Brady decided to ride to the basin

immediately in order to make sure that the women were there, before speaking to Willard Duff. When he drew near to the basin, he approached it cautiously, but not cautiously enough to avoid the sharp eyes of Debbie Randle, concealed near the rim of the hollow. She ran down to the others.

'He's coming!' she shouted.

When Brady peered cautiously down over the brim he saw the six women seated by the campfire, talking with one another, with no indication that they were intending to leave in the near future. Eager to give Duff the news, he stayed only a few minutes, then headed for the ranch.

Thirty minutes later, the women left the basin and rode to the ravine where they had previously been held prisoner. They took a route over which it would be impossible for their tracks to be followed.

In the grove by the river, Jack and the others saw Brady ride up fast to the ranch house, dismount, and disappear from view.

Moments later they saw him and the two Duffs standing in front of the ranch house. Willard Duff, who had decided to expedite matters by seizing this opportunity to capture the women now, rather than wait for them to turn up at the ranch was shouting to his men.

Jack and Randle prepared to leave.

'Stay here,' said Jack to the others, 'unless you hear gunfire. If you do, we could probably do with some help.'

Carrying some rope, the two men slipped out of the grove and over the river bank, to stand in the water. The river was running low at the time. Crouching below the top of the bank, they walked along the river bed until they were directly behind the ranch house.

Then, screened by the ranch house itself, they ran up to a door in the rear of the house, which Jack had noticed on a previous visit. The success of Jack's plan depended entirely on whether or not they could open this door from the outside.

He grasped the handle, turned it, and pushed. The door opened silently and he and Randle slipped inside. Cautiously, they checked the ground floor. It appeared to be unoccupied. They could hear Duff's voice, still barking orders, outside.

Silently, they climbed up the stairs. There appeared to be three bedroom doors, one of which was open. Creeping up to it, Jack peered into the room. Green, with his back to Jack, was standing at the window, viewing the activity outside. Danny, his hands and feet tied, was lying on the bed.

The boy saw Jack, who raised his finger to his lips, then crept up behind Green and stunned him with a blow to the head from the barrel of his pistol. Before the Box D hand had recovered, Jack and Randle had quickly gagged and blindfolded him, and tied him so tightly that he was incapable of raising the alarm.

They cut the ropes around Danny's hands and feet, then all three of them crept down the stairs and out of the back door of the house. There were sounds of activity on the other side of the house, as they retraced the path which Jack and Randle had previously followed, and rejoined the settlers waiting for them in the grove.

Then, making sure they were not observed, they headed for the ravine where the women were waiting for them. It was an hour before the men at the ranch realized that Danny was missing.

Fifteen minutes after Jack and Randle had left with Danny, the two Duffs, with fifteen hands, rode off towards the hollow where Brady had seen the women. But when they arrived there, the hollow was empty. Nor could they find clear tracks to enable them to follow the women. The rancher decided to return to the Box D.

On the way back they were met by a hand who told them that Danny had been rescued by someone unknown. Furious at being outwitted, the rancher wondered who had rescued the boy. He called Blaney over and took him aside.

'Go to the canyon,' he said, 'and check that that cave entrance is still blocked like it was when we left.'

When Blaney returned to the ranch house some time later, he reported that the blockage of the cave entrance was still intact.

Willard Duff paced up and down in his living-room, wondering what his next move should be. Eventually, he called his son in.

'Brad,' he said. 'We know those settlers' wives are around somewhere. We've got to find them. Take some men into town and make sure the women ain't there. Then we'll start looking outside town for them. They might have gone to Tipawa to the children, but I doubt it. I think they're somewhere nearer than that. Maybe they've got some crazy notion of taking revenge for what they think we've done to their menfolk.'

Brad Duff returned during the evening to tell his father that there was no sign of the women in Monroe.

'Right,' said his father, 'we'll decide in the morning what to do next.'

When Danny arrived at the ravine with Jack and the other men, his mother ran to meet and hug him, and there was general rejoicing among the homesteaders over the reunion. Jack congratulated Leary on his successful hoodwinking of Brady.

After taking a meal they settled down to discuss the second phase of the plan, which was to start the following day.

Leary was an interested listener, disappointed that on this occasion there was no part for him to play.

Jack spent some time with Miriam and Danny when the discussion was over. The boy, a sturdy youngster, seemed to have recovered well from his ordeal. He asked Jack when they would be able to go back to the homestead.

'Pretty soon, I hope, Danny,' Jack replied. 'It all depends on how our plan goes tomorrow.'

'You'll be coming with us?' asked the boy, hopefully. 'I was figuring you might teach me a bit about guns, for when I get older. And we sure need some help on the home-stead.'

'That's up to your mother, Danny,' said Jack. 'I ain't got no other place to go to just now.'

Miriam smiled. 'We're grateful,' she said, 'for what you've done for us up to now, and if we get the better of Duff I'll be more than glad for you to stay on.'

Jack asked Danny if he knew the names of the two men who had kidnapped him.

'Yes,' replied the boy. 'They were Jackson and Barclay.'

Shortly after this, Miriam sent Danny off to get some sleep. She and Jack sat in silence for a while. Then Jack spoke.

'I guess you've been wondering, Miriam,' he said, 'how an ex-lawman like myself came to be drifting through these parts. It's still hard for me to talk about what hap-pened, but I'd like you to know.'

Speaking slowly, he told her the story of how, as marshal of a Kansas cattle town, he had arrested two outlaws who had been sentenced to long terms of imprisonment in the State Penitentiary. The two men had escaped and had attacked him and his wife in his own home.

He had wounded the two men, and in return had received only a minor wound himself, but in the course of the gun battle his pregnant wife had been killed instantly by a bullet from the gun of one of the outlaws. Both the outlaws had subsequently been hanged.

He himself had been devastated by the loss of his wife and unborn child, and had quit his job and drifted aimlessly until he had met Miriam and had found some purpose to his life again.

'I guess you know how I felt,' he said, 'having lost your own husband the way you did.'

'You're right,' said Miriam, 'but life goes on, and I've got Danny to think of.'

Jack rode into Monroe after dark to see Ranger and tell him about the rescue of

Danny. He also discussed with him their plans for the following day. Then he returned to the ravine.

Early the next morning, before daybreak, Jack and the five settlers rode into town and up to the livery stable from the rear. Hal Reynolds, who was waiting for them, showed them into a small storeroom at the rear of the stable and put their horses away. The men, faced with a wait of a few hours, sat down and tried to relax.

At a quarter to ten, Miriam and the other five women rode slowly into town, passing close by Harker, sitting on his porch. His eyes goggled and he stood up, then moved out into the street to watch the six riders as they dismounted at the store and went through the door leading to the living-quarters.

From inside the stable, Reynolds watched Harker, who hurriedly entered his shack and emerged a few minutes later. The old-timer started walking along the boardwalk towards the livery stable. Then he spotted

Miller, a Box D hand, cantering into town alone, and hailed him.

Reynolds saw the two men exchange a few hurried words, after which Miller turned and rode out of town, while Harker returned to his porch.

Reynolds told Jack and the others that a Box D rider had just left town, almost certainly to tell Duff that the women homesteaders were in the storekeeper's house. Then he gave the same information to Ranger.

Thirty minutes later, May Dixon, Debbie Randle and Ruth Lee left through a side door of the store, which was not in sight of Harker sitting in his porch along the street. They entered the saloon from the rear.

At the same time, Ellen Fisher and Ethel Grant climbed the stairs to the second floor of the storekeeper's living-quarters.

A further twenty minutes passed before the two Duffs, with fifteen hands, were spotted, riding fast towards town. The riders slowed down as they reached the first buildings, then came to a stop outside the store. The street was deserted.

The rancher was just about to call on the storekeeper to come outside, when a movement at one of the two store windows which faced on to the street caught his eye.

The barrels of a double-barrelled shotgun had been poked out of the open window, and were pointing in his direction. Behind the shotgun was the grim face of Will Ranger. A moment later, a shotgun appeared in the other window, in the hands of Miriam Farrell, and two rifle barrels appeared in the windows of the two bedrooms above the store.

Nervously, the rancher looked around. His worst fears were realized. Two rifle barrels and one shotgun barrel were projecting from the three windows of the saloon, and Hal Reynolds, standing just inside the livery stable door, was pointing a double-barrelled shotgun in his direction. Standing by his side, holding a rifle, was the doctor.

The array of artillery they were facing had

not gone unnoticed by Brad Duff and the Box D hands. They looked uncertainly at the rancher.

Willard Duff cleared his throat.

'Don't start anything,' he ordered, knowing that if they did they would likely be cut to pieces. 'And stay on your horses.'

Movement at the entrance to the livery stable caught his eye and he stared in utter disbelief as Jack walked out on to the street with the five homesteaders, all holding six-guns in their hands. Slowly, they walked side by side towards the mounted men and stopped well clear of the rancher, outside the blast pattern of the shotguns, should they be fired.

'What I want you all to do,' said Jack, 'is unbuckle your gun belts and drop them on the ground. Then drop your rifles down as well. And better be quick about it. There's quite a few folk with itchy trigger-fingers holding guns on you right now.'

'Do it!' said the rancher, and Jack's instructions were quickly obeyed.

From the store and the saloon, Miriam and the other women came out and walked over to stand by the men, facing the rancher.

'This is the end for you, Duff,' said Jack. 'Just because there's no lawman around here, you reckoned you could make your own laws. That was a big mistake. We're going to take you to the law ourselves.

'You masterminded the whole operation. You caused the death of Benson the prospector, and you helped in the attempted murder of myself and these men with me. You ordered the capture of the women by Daley and his men.

'We also aim to hand over to the law that son of yours and Blaney, who helped you to seal us in that cave; and Barclay and Jackson, who kidnapped young Danny Farrell in Tipawa.

'As for the death of Clem Farrell, we're pretty sure you're responsible for that too, and maybe we can prove it before you come to trial.

213

'As for the rest of you, we're going to hold you here for twenty-four hours before we let you go. By that time we'll be well on the way to handing Duff and the others over to the law. There'll be no more pay coming from Duff here, and maybe the law'll want to talk to you about some of the things you've been doing for him. If I was you, I wouldn't stay around here for too long.'

The two Duffs, with Blaney, Jackson and Barclay, were ordered to dismount and their hands were bound. The remaining men from the Box D were then told to dismount and were taken to the old Norton house and ordered through the trapdoor into the underground room. The women would stand guard over them until they were released.

'I wouldn't try to get out,' advised Jack. 'There'll be a couple of shotguns trained on that trapdoor, around the clock.'

Jack and the men settlers set off for Amarillo within the hour, escorting the two Duffs and their three hands. Before leaving, it was arranged that the women, as soon as the prisoners were released, would ride to Tipawa with Danny to collect the children there, and would then go back to their homesteads to await the return of the men from Amarillo.

Before his wife had been murdered, Jack had been friendly with a Kansas lawman, Phil Burton, who had moved to a post in Amarillo as US Marshal. He hoped that Burton was still there.

THIRTEEN

The ride to Amarillo, with two nights camped out on the trail, proved uneventful. When they halted outside the US Marshal's office in Amarillo, and Jack dismounted and walked through the door, he was pleased to see his old friend Phil Burton seated at the desk inside.

Burton was a tall, slim, hawk-faced man of middle age, wearing a neatly-trimmed moustache. Seeing Jack, he jumped to his feet and walked round the desk to greet him.

'Jack!' he said. 'I've been worried about you. I heard about Beth and tried to get in touch with you, but nobody knew where you were.'

'I had a bad time, Phil,' said Jack, 'but I reckon I've sorted myself out at last.'

He went on to tell Burton about the criminal activities of the prisoners he had outside. The marshal listened with interest.

'I'm hoping,' he said, when Jack had finished, 'that it won't be long before there are plenty of law officers around to make sure this sort of thing can't happen.'

He called a deputy to put the prisoners in a cell at the rear of the building. Then Jack introduced Burton to his companions, before they all sat down with him to provide details of the offences that the prisoners had committed.

'We have a judge in town,' said Burton. 'He'll try this case tomorrow. We'll need the testimony of you and your friends, of course. Then you can all go back and lick those quarter sections into shape again.'

During cross-examination at the trial, Blaney revealed that, on Willard Duff's orders, Clem Farrell, Miriam's husband, had been murdered by the half-breed Parker, now dead.

At the end of the trial, Willard Duff was

sentenced to death by hanging. Brad Duff and Blaney received long custodial sentences. Shorter sentences were imposed on Jackson and Barclay.

When the trial was over Jack and his companions headed for the homesteads.

When the women arrived in Tipawa, the whole town turned out to greet them. They cheered at the women's account of the downfall of Willard Duff.

Henry Baxter told them that two US deputy marshals, with a jail wagon, had collected the Daley gang the previous day. The deputies had told him that there was a reward of 9,000 dollars payable for the handing over to the law of the four members of the gang.

It had been agreed with Baxter that a deputy would hand him the reward money in about a week's time. Baxter would then get his son Nat to take the money to Miriam on her homestead. She could then divide it among the six families.

The women were excited at the prospect of receiving a sum of money, large indeed to them, which would help greatly to ease the burden of frontier life.

They left Tipawa with the children the following day, with the whole town assembled to say goodbye and wish them well. Four days after they reached the homesteads they were joined by Jack and the others.

It took them all a couple of weeks' hard work, after the period of neglect, to get the quarter sections back into shape. Halfway through the second week, Nat Baxter rode in with the reward money, and Miriam handed 1,500 dollars to each of the other five families.

One evening a few days later, after Danny had gone to bed, Jack and Miriam sat talking in the living-room.

'I've been thinking, Miriam,' said Jack. 'You and me, we seem to hit it off pretty good, don't we?'

'That's right,' she said, wondering what

was coming.

'The last thing my wife Beth would have wanted,' said Jack, 'would be for me to live the life of a lonely man. And I guess your husband Clem might have felt the same way about you being left on your own.

'I like being around you and Danny, and you're the sort of woman I admire. I've been wondering if you could ever entertain the notion of us two getting married?'

She smiled at him.

'You're a good man, Jack Nelson,' she said, 'and I think that what you said about Clem is dead right. Danny and me, we need a man around. And Danny looks up to you. Even though Clem ain't been dead that long, I think that getting hitched is the right thing for us to do. At least it would stop people talking.'

'I'm glad you're in favour of the idea,' said Jack. 'Now I've got two things to ask you before we go ahead.'

'Oh yes,' said Miriam. 'What would they be?'

'First,' said Jack, 'tell me whether you're liable to hit me on the head with a mallet if ever I step out of line?'

Miriam smiled.

'Only if you take a real big step out of line,' she replied, 'and I'm sure that ain't likely to happen.'

'Right,' said Jack, 'and second, I didn't mention before that I own a ranch in Kansas, not far from Dodge City, that's being run for me by a friend of mine for as long as I ain't ready to take it over myself. What d'you think of the idea of the three of us moving over there and running the place?'

Miriam considered the proposal, which came as something of a shock to her. Then she replied,

'My memories of this place ain't good,' she said. 'I think a fresh start would be a good thing for Danny and me. And I know that the Grants want to add some more land on to their quarter section. This place would probably suit them fine. Let's leave as soon as we can fix it.'

They kissed, and two weeks later they were married. Three days after the wedding, they left the valley with Danny, heading for the Bar N Ranch in Kansas.

The publishers hope that this book has given you enjoyable reading. Large Print Books are especially designed to be as easy to see and hold as possible. If you wish a complete list of our books please ask at your local library or write directly to:

Dales Large Print Books
Magna House, Long Preston,
Skipton, North Yorkshire.
BD23 4ND

This Large Print Book, for people
who cannot read normal print,
is published under the auspices of
THE ULVERSCROFT FOUNDATION

... we hope you have enjoyed this book.
Please think for a moment about those
who have worse eyesight than you ...
and are unable to even read or enjoy
Large Print without great difficulty.

You can help them by sending a
donation, large or small, to:

**The Ulverscroft Foundation,
1, The Green, Bradgate Road,
Anstey, Leicestershire, LE7 7FU,
England.**
or request a copy of our brochure for
more details.

The Foundation will use all donations
to assist those people who are visually
impaired and need special attention
with medical research, diagnosis
and treatment.

Thank you very much for your help.